F York
YOR   The ghost of the
       Isherwoods

DATE DUE

228	9	411 M.V	JAN 28 '81
332	22	116 FI	MAY 25 '83
309	APR 13	311 JN	OCT 21 '85
204	MAY 29 '73	104 MF	FEB 25 '88
438	APR 3	605 EB	NOV 2 '88
5 01	JUN 22 '73	110 MJ	OCT 8 '91
308	OCT 2 '74	806 DC	JAN 16 '92
537	OCT 21 '74	5SL	NOV 0 4 1999
307	NOV 13 '74	7 AY	APR 8 3 2001
308	APR 16 '75	7 MU	MAY 0 5 2002
301	APR 30 '75	6 RS	AUG 2 2
	77		

THE GHOST OF
THE ISHERWOODS

The Ghost of
THE ISHERWOODS

CAROL BEACH YORK

Franklin Watts, Inc.
575 Lexington Avenue
New York, N.Y. 10022

Second Printing

Copyright © 1966 by Franklin Watts, Inc.
Library of Congress Catalog Card Number: 66–12120
Printed in the United States of America

To a dear friend,
MARIAN ROBERTS

THE GHOST OF
THE ISHERWOODS

CHAPTER ONE

THERE DID NOT SEEM to be anything strange about the house at first. Sunlight fell across the floor of the large entry hall. Behind us, through the open door, came the fragrance of oleander in the garden; before us, a wide staircase led upward with a gleaming curve of mahogany banister.

"Isn't it lovely," my mother said, standing behind me with her white-gloved hands on my shoulders.

The thin, gray-haired woman who had let us in stood blinking silently as Daddy and Don and Ritchie Allen set our suitcases down around her, until she seemed to be marooned behind them in her corner by the door. We heard a phone receiver being put back into place, and then Aunt Vivian came hurrying from a room at one side of the hall, arms outstretched to greet us, high heels clicking on the polished floor.

"Hello! Hello!" she cried, enveloping us all in the warmth of her welcome and the exotic sweetness of her perfume. She looked very gay and cool in a silky green dress splashed with a swirling design of white flowers. Her fingers were full of rings, and from one hand floated a huge chiffon handkerchief, which she

1

occasionally flourished in front of her face like a fan. She quickly kissed Mother and me, putting her cheek by ours and puckering her lips into the air above our ears—oh, she did smell wonderful! She gave Daddy a dazzling smile, and extended one hand to Don and one to Ritchie Allen.

"Donald—handsome as ever," she declared. "And you must be Ritchie," she went on, welcoming him as heartily as she welcomed the rest of us. "You go to school with Don, don't you? I am so happy you could come."

"It's nice of you to invite me," Ritchie said, with what Mother called his "lovely manners"—but I looked away. I'd been staring again. It was always hard for me not to stare at Ritchie Allen; he had such a handsome, lean, graceful look about him, such long, dark lashes and dark, tumbling hair.

I think Aunt Vivian was a little startled at how good-looking he was, for she laughed softly, holding the boys' hands in hers a moment longer as she said, "You two will have all the girls in town hanging around here before the week's over."

Then she turned away from them easily, knowing just the right moment to stop teasing so that they wouldn't be embarrassed. (Though nothing ever embarrassed my brother Don; he was very blond and handsome, and he probably thought exactly the same thing himself—that he would soon have all the girls in town clamoring to go out with him; oh, the hearts he would break in his week's visit! As for Ritchie, I couldn't guess what he thought of Aunt Vivian's remark, but he was more serious than Don, and I think he used to think about other things than girls at least once in a while.)

"This is Mrs. Lockley," Aunt Vivian said, introducing the woman who had answered the door and stood a little aside, among the suitcases. She had on a plain dark cotton dress and cotton apron; her only ornament was a small pearl brooch pinned to the front of her dress. She nodded around at us as Aunt Vivian named us one by one. "This is my sister, Mrs. Abbott," Aunt Vivian began with Mother; "and this is Mr. Abbott, and this darling,"—here she gave me a squeeze—"this is Louise. Isn't she precious? And my nephew, Donald, and his friend, Ritchie Allen."

Then Aunt Vivian turned to us and said enthusiastically, "Mrs. Lockley is the best housekeeper I've ever had. I could never have gotten along without her."

Aunt Vivian always introduced people with superlatives. Every maid, cook, gardener, or housekeeper she had ever had as long as I could remember had been, each in his turn, *the* best! Mother said that it was a nice relief from the complaining you so often heard from people about their household help.

We all smiled politely at Mrs. Lockley, who looked a little less thin and dry under the glow of Aunt Vivian's words.

"This is a lovely place," Daddy said to Aunt Vivian.

3

"Oh, thank you, Charles," she said. "But come along, you haven't seen it all yet—come along, come along—leave the suitcases." She put her arm around my shoulders and motioned for everyone to follow as she led the way to show us the rest of the house.

The living room and the library were at opposite sides of the entrance hall. The living room, with Aunt Vivian's rose-colored sofas facing each other before a wide fireplace, led to an ornate dining room dominated by heavy walnut furnishings and a long breakfront displaying Aunt Vivian's stemware and china. A large old-fashioned kitchen stretched across the back of the house and opened onto a screened porch. Opposite the kitchen there was a pantry-storeroom and a flight of worn steps leading down to the cellar and up to the second floor.

The library was a darkish, comfortable room with leather chairs; Uncle Arthur's desk with burnished brass handles on the drawers; and a large globe in a floor stand—ideal for staring at thoughtfully and giving a spin to now and then as you talked. French doors opened to a small flagstone terrace and a walled garden. Here, beyond the flagstones and the green lawn and the flowerbeds, foliage was thick and overgrown, with a dark, tangled look. Vines hung along the wall, and for perhaps twenty feet, between lawn and wall, bushes and brambles and untended strange plants grew so close together that it looked almost impossible to walk through them to the wall. On the lawn was a stone birdbath, reflecting a crisscross of tree branches and blue sky in its calm surface. But there were no birds in the garden then, and I never saw or heard one there during all the days of our visit.

On the terrace was a small iron bench, and at each side of the terrace two small gray stone horses with wings cast midafternoon shadows easterly across the flagstones. To these apparently quite old and permanent fixtures, several folding lawn chairs had been added and a metal table covered by a gigantic green umbrella with a deep, white fringe.

"Oh, Vivian, it's all so charming." Mother sighed with pleasure, absorbed by the tangling foliage and the terrace and the stone horses. "How can you bear to part with it?"

"*I* can't really," Aunt Vivian answered. Her tone faintly suggested that there was someone else who could bear to part with it, even though she couldn't.

"Do you *have* to sell it?" I asked impulsively, and Aunt Vivian said, "I'm afraid so, sweetie." Everyone was silent a moment, and I felt that they all thought me silly for asking such a question. I knew that Uncle Arthur had accepted a business transfer to California. Whether they sold this house first or not, they would be leaving soon for the house in California which Uncle Arthur had already found for them.

"I really will miss it." Aunt Vivian fingered the filmy handkerchief gently. "This year has gone so fast. We never dreamed when we bought the house that we'd only have it a year. It's such a lovely house, and I'm so glad you could all come and visit before we have to leave. Imagine," she added less solemnly, "not just one guest room, but two, and a small room that I use for sewing, which can also serve as a temporary guest room. It'd be a pity not to use them at least once."

Beyond the wall, we could hear the noises of the town, faint, muted, undisturbing. Along the quiet residential streets there had not been much activity when we came. I could picture the streets on the other side of the wall—peaceful, shady, lazy on a summer afternoon . . . Turning, I saw Mrs. Lockley watching us from the terrace doors. For a moment, before Aunt Vivian saw her and spoke to her, there was a troubled expression on the housekeeper's face; and then I realized that she was not actually looking at us, but past us, into the shrubbery and tall grass and twining ivy that grew along the wall. Her eyes squinted as if she were trying to see something there that she couldn't quite make out.

"Did you want something, Mrs. Lockley?" Aunt Vivian saw her just then and took a step toward the doors. Mrs. Lockley came out onto the terrace.

"It's just that Jessie called to see if the company was here yet," Mrs. Lockley said. "She's on her way home."

"Running all the way at top speed, I suppose." Aunt Vivian sighed and shook her head. Then she said to Mother, "I've about given up trying to get Jessie to be dignified and ladylike. She was so restless waiting for all of you this afternoon that I said: 'Jessie, please go and *do* something'; so she decided to visit one of her girl friends for awhile. She'll probably come bolting in soon, out of breath and dripping with perspiration. It's certainly too hot to run anywhere today." Aunt Vivian fanned herself with the handkerchief to emphasize this.

Mother laughed. "Jessie's just a child, Vivian. You have a lot of time to make her dignified."

Even Daddy was chuckling to himself at the vision of my cousin Jessie being dignified.

"She's twelve already," Aunt Vivian protested. "My goodness, when we were twelve—why, don't you remember, Winifred, *we* were *very* dignified, interested in boys, and learning social dancing at school, as I recall."

"I know, I know." Mother nodded, laughing again. "We thought we were rather grown-up."

"Oh, I'm not fair," Aunt Vivian said suddenly. "Jessie's improving quite a bit. She's even interested in boys a little, I think. Well, come in and I'll show you your rooms and then we'll have some nice cool lemonade."

Aunt Vivian took me into the lead again, since I was handiest. She tucked her arm through mine, and everyone followed in her wake back through the French doors into the library, blinking in the dimness after being out in the sun-filled garden. Mrs.

7

Lockley had disappeared as quietly as she had come.

The library was empty and the door at the opposite side of the room stood open to the front hall and our suitcases by the door. I had the impression that someone was there, but when we came through the library into the hall, it, too, was empty.

"How old are you now, Louise?" Aunt Vivian asked. "I'm always losing track. You're all growing up so fast."

"Fifteen," I answered—not very loudly. Ritchie Allen was eighteen, and I was always hoping that he would forget I was three years younger.

"What was that, dear?" Aunt Vivian bent toward me with a rustle of silk.

"Fifteen," I answered, a bit more loudly. I noticed with relief that Ritchie and Don were lingering behind in the library, taking another look around at the walls of books.

"Yes, of course. Fifteen." Aunt Vivian nodded her head agreeably. "All of you children are growing up *so* fast. Why, I guess Marcella must be sixteen then." She turned to include Mother and Daddy as she continued. "That reminds me, I forgot to tell you that I called Sybil on the spur of the moment the other night, to see if she and Marcella couldn't come for a few days, too. But you know how Sybil is, always so busy with her shop. She said that perhaps Marcella could come though, when her modeling class finishes its summer term, which I guess is this week or next."

8

"It's too bad Sybil can't get away," Mother murmured.

My heart sank. It had never occurred to me that Aunt Vivian might invite Aunt Sybil and Marcella to come. Aunt Vivian went on chattering merrily. "I hope Marcella does come. She can swim and play tennis. She needs to get outdoors more. She leads much too grown-up a life for her age—helping in the hat shop after school, taking modeling lessons all summer. Listen to me, fussing one minute because Jessie won't be dignified and ladylike, and then criticizing my sister Sybil because her daughter is too grown-up and dignified."

"Well, there has to be a happy medium, I guess," Daddy said.

Aunt Vivian seized the opportunity to give me another squeeze and said, "I think Louise is our happy medium."

I smiled weakly. I didn't want to be the happy medium at all. I wanted to be sophisticated and take modeling lessons just exactly like Cousin Marcella. But every time I asked Mother about it she put me off with answers like, "You're only fifteen, Louise," or, "You're not old enough to worry about being sophisticated yet." But I *was* old enough and I *did* worry about being sophisticated. I'd worried *especially* since last Christmastime when Don brought Ritchie Allen home from college with him to spend the holiday with us. No sooner had the boys arrived than Marcella and Aunt Sybil came for two days. (Aunt Sybil is a widow and the Christmas holidays always make her blue, so usually she closes up her hat shop and comes to visit us awhile.) So there was Marcella, so grown-up and glamorous, strutting about and striking poses that she'd learned at modeling school. Ritchie thought Marcella was wonderful. I watched unhappily as he followed her around and tried to open doors for her and hold her coat and things like that. And Marcella thought Ritchie was wonderful, and rolled her eyes at him and talked about her modeling school. *Finally*, she and Aunt Sybil left, in a flurry of fur pieces and hat boxes and fine, misty snow. And I had hoped ever since that Marcella and Ritchie Allen would never meet again. *I hope she doesn't come,* I told myself fiercely. *Louise Abbott, what a dreadful thing to think,* I scolded myself half-heartedly. *Anyway, maybe she won't be able to come for some reason or other, and you're just worrying for nothing.* Nevertheless, my heart had sunk . . . Aunt Vivian was saying, "Now let's get the suitcases upstairs and I'll show you your rooms."

Everyone took something, and we went up the wide, curving stairs, our steps silent on the thick carpeting. A clock in the hall below struck three as we reached the top and stood facing the long upstairs hall. A single window at the far end sent a shaft of light straight along the floor to our feet, and we could see the top of the backstairs railing showing at the corner of the hall. Behind us, stretching across the front of the house, were two rooms, Aunt Vivian and Uncle Arthur's room and a guest room.

"That's our room, over there," Aunt Vivian said, motioning to one of the rooms, "and this is for you and Charles, Winifred." Mother and Daddy went in, and the rest of us clustered in the doorway, looking admiringly around at the pretty white and lavender room with bowls of pink dianthuses at each side of the windows. Aunt Vivian stepped in briskly, opened closet doors, and straightened the dresser scarf. "I'm sure you'll find enough room. Just make yourselves at home, and change into something cool and comfortable for supper."

"Come along, sweetie," she said to me, and Don and Ritchie followed as we went along the hall. "This is Jessie's room," Aunt Vivian said at the first door, and again she hurried in briskly. "She's cleared out half the closet for you—well, almost." Aunt Vivian had opened the door and stood frowning at a jumble of tennis shoes and rackets, bedroom slippers and magazines piled up on the closet floor. However, the clothes rack *was* almost half bare, and there had been a serious attempt to clear some space for me on the shelf above. I thought Jessie had done very well.

"It's fine," I assured Aunt Vivian, who seemed to prefer anything to an encounter with the jumble of things on the closet floor. She looked relieved. "Well, we'll see," she said vaguely, and went off to show

11

Don and Ritchie to the second guest room, which was across the hall.

I set my suitcase on the bed and snapped it open. As I began to take out some of the things folded near the top, shaking out wrinkles, I could see evidence of my cousin Jessie everywhere around the room. I think I would have known it was her room if I had been led to it blindfolded across the desert. There was a pile of books on the only chair, which was drawn over by the windows and had a bag of potato chips only half hidden from sight under one side. There was a phonograph and a stack of records on a table by the bed. On the dresser were more magazines and books, a bathing cap with the strap missing, and, despite Aunt Vivian's protests that Jessie was not ladylike, two tubes of lipstick—very pale shades, I discovered, uncapping them and twisting them up to see. Just right for about twelve years old.

I hung my dresses on some empty hangers that I found in the closet. They didn't begin to take up all the space, so I eased some of Jessie's clothes back from their crowded half of the bar.

Then, thinking I might be able to see Jessie coming, I went to the windows. I could see down to the terrace and the lawn, and from that height I could see over the wall—where the trees did not block the view—and into the street opposite. A group of children came riding by slowly on bicycles, and stopped to have a conference at the corner across from my window. A car or two went by, but there was no one else in sight along the street. I sat down for a moment by the window, resting my arms along the sill and looking down at the stone horses and the silent garden. It was such a nice house, such a pretty garden; I wished I were very rich, so I could buy it— and I wondered who would buy it, and who would live there.

The house had belonged to some friends of Uncle Arthur and Aunt Vivian's, and I remembered Aunt Vivian writing Mother a long, excited letter about the house the fall before. The Carew family had decided to sell the house and move to Florida, and although it was more room than Uncle Arthur and Aunt Vivian and Jessie needed they had decided to buy it. "I can hardly wait for you to come next summer and see it," Aunt Vivian had written. But then when summer came, Uncle Arthur had accepted the transfer to California and Aunt Vivian had written, "We'll move as soon as we can sell this house or at the end of August, whichever comes first; just so Jessie will be in California when the school year starts."

So we had not planned to visit Aunt Vivian and Uncle Arthur this summer, and the summer seemed to be dragging along uneventfully until Don decided to invite Ritchie Allen to come and spend a few weeks with us. Ritchie had been at our house for about ten days when Aunt Vivian called long-distance to say that they hadn't sold the house so far, and therefore they would be staying until the end of August. So would we come for a week's visit after all? Aunt Vivian asked. When the phone rang, I was sitting at the kitchen table eating a sandwich and kicking my feet against the rungs of the chair because Don and Ritchie had gone out somewhere without me and I was hot and bored. I listened to Mother's part of the conversation, which began: "We'd love to come, of course . . . I'm just thinking; you see, Don has a school friend here—we thought we'd be home all summer. He's a very nice boy. We met him when Don brought him home at Christmas. He only has his father, who travels most of the time—I think he's away from home now. He was counting on Ritchie staying with us until it was time for the boys to go back to school."

I certainly pricked up my ears when I heard this. How awful it would be to say, "Sorry, Ritchie, we're all going away after all, so you'll have to go home." Why, it seemed like he had *just* come. But apparently Aunt Vivian was insisting that there was plenty of room at her house for Ritchie Allen to come along too, because next I heard Mother making feeble protests that this might be an imposition on Aunt Vivian. As soon as I heard the tone of Mother's voice I knew she wanted to go, and I began mentally sorting over my clothes to decide what I would take—and I was half packed, in my mind, when Mother finally hung up the telephone and

14

came out to the kitchen and said, "Guess what, Louise."

It seemed right to be going, I thought; we had visited Aunt Vivian and Uncle Arthur and Jessie for a week every summer since I could remember. We knew their town, their streets and stores and neighborhood nearly as well as we knew our own. Jessie and Don and I would walk along together to the movies on hot afternoons; or take our bathing suits to the Westriver Park pool; or sit playing Monopoly and Scrabble on the front porch swing of the big, rambling white frame house they had lived in since Jessie was born. But of course this house they had recently bought, this part of town, were new to us now. Aunt Vivian and Uncle Arthur had lived in another section of town before, closer to the shops and businesses. This house, this street, and this part of town took getting used to, getting to know all over again, like a strange place. I wondered if we would still go to Westriver Park to swim, or if it was too far now to walk uptown to see a movie.

In the street beyond the wall, the children rode away on their bicycles until I could not see them anymore. There was no one else in sight either way along the street. Suddenly I was aware that the sun was gone. I stood up, shivering for no reason, and turned around quickly as someone who feels that he is being watched does. There was nothing but the empty room, and I wondered why I had suddenly felt an eeriness around me; it was probably no more than the passing of a cloud before the sun. Yet below my window the lawn and terrace lay in a cheerless gray light, and a cat, black but for two yellow eyes, had come onto the terrace and sat by the iron bench as motionless as the stone horses with their stone wings.

Then I heard voices in the hall as my cousin Jessie ran up the stairs and spoke to Mother and Daddy. A moment later she appeared at the doorway, long dark hair streaming from the security of a plastic hair-band, breathless and laughing because she had run so fast to see us all and was so happy that we were there.

"Hi, Jessie," I said, suddenly glad not to be alone in the room.

"Hi," she answered, and ran over to give me a hug. "I'll help you unpack," she offered eagerly, catching sight of my open suitcase on the bed. "Oh, this is darling—" and she picked up a pink housecoat lying in my suitcase and held it up in front of herself to see how it looked.

Jessie always liked to see everything that was in the suitcases when we came. When she had been younger she had run back and forth from my suitcase to Mother's, and Mother always had something for her tucked away at the bottom for a surprise. For the time being, Jessie seemed content to stay with me, and she sat on the bed beside the suitcase and tried on my bracelets and my new gloves and my white pumps, while I put pajamas and shorts and blouses in the dresser drawer and found room among the magazines on the dresser for my hairbrush and cold cream and nail polish.

Aunt Vivian came back after a few minutes to see how I was getting along. She playfully chided Jessie for having on all my things, and told her to change into a fresh dress before supper. Jessie was wearing a blue blouse and a pair of once-white shorts, below which her bony little knees showed a variety of scratches and mosquito bites. Obediently she took off my shoes and bracelets and went to the closet for a dress. Aunt Vivian walked to the window and said, "I think it's going to rain. It's gotten quite cloudy."

Jessie laid her dress on the bed and began to unbutton her blouse. She stood close to me, staring past her mother toward the sunless afternoon. Then she said to me, "Do you like this house, Louise?"

Before I could answer, Aunt Vivian turned around from the window and said, "Now, Jessie, don't start bothering everyone with your spooky stories."

"But, Mother, I only asked her if she liked the house," Jessie protested.

"You know what I mean," Aunt Vivian said firmly. Then she flourished her handkerchief at Jessie and said, "And don't look so creepy; you'll scare everyone."

"But, Mother——" Jessie began to protest again,

17

but Aunt Vivian interrupted her in a serious tone: "This is a perfectly nice, normal house, Jessie. Now you know that."

For the moment both of them seemed to have forgotten me entirely, and stood looking steadily at each other. Jessie looked away first, lowering her eyes at last to the buttons on her blouse. Then Aunt Vivian remembered me and exclaimed, "Don't pay any attention to Jessie, dear. She lets her imagination run away with her sometimes. She thinks this house is spooky, but don't let her scare you."

"It is *so* spooky," Jessie muttered, and Aunt Vivian made a low moan of exasperation.

"There's a legend, too," Jessie said. "There really is, Louise. A legend about a ghost that——"

"A ghost. Oh, Jessie," Aunt Vivian said, "there aren't any such things." She stood with her head on one side, regarding Jessie with a baffled expression.

"Mrs. Lockley told me," Jessie insisted.

"Yes, I know." Aunt Vivian waved her handkerchief in a last helpless gesture. "That's just a story, Jessie. I've told you before, I don't want you talking about it anymore. Now, my goodness, what a way to begin Louise's visit!" She gave me a quick affectionate pat to make up for this beginning to my visit. "Now you two come downstairs when you're ready and have some lemonade. Don't forget to brush your hair, Jessie."

"I won't," Jessie answered absently. And when Aunt Vivian had gone, she whispered to me, "There

18

really is a legend about a ghost, Louise. Mrs. Lockley told me. We'll go downstairs and find her and she'll tell it again for you. It's a really true story. . . ." As she talked she put on the clean dress and pulled the hairbrush through her hair once or twice.

I looked down to the terrace again, but the black cat was gone. I wanted to play with it, and I wondered where it had gone. Jessie, dressed and ready, came and stood beside me at the window.

"I'm glad we're selling this house," she said. And then she added softly, "You'll see."

CHAPTER TWO

So THERE DIDN'T seem to be anything strange about the house at first—but that was only the brief deception of sun and flowers, of greeting each other with kisses and exclamations of pleasure. Those were the ordinary, everyday things, like a bright surface over the hours; beneath was some strange, less pleasant current. The feeling that someone or something watched me in quiet moments, in empty rooms, persisted as long as I was in that house, where there were no birds in the garden and where no one ever wanted to stay alone.

As for the sun that had cast such reassurance upon our arrival, shining on the floor of the hall, reflecting in the placid water of the birdbath, we had seen the last of it for several days to come. So the grown-ups thought it was only the dreariness of the cloudy days that oppressed the atmosphere—or at least they would not admit to *us* that it was anything else.

Cousin Jessie wanted me to hear Mrs. Lockley's story, and she led me down by the back stairway to the kitchen, so we wouldn't be intercepted by our parents. We could hear their voices in the living room, where they had gathered to have lemonade, and we caught a glimpse of Mrs. Lockley in the passageway as she went toward the living room with a tray of glasses and a plate of tea cakes with pink frosting. I was hungry and I thought about how good some tea cakes would taste, each one only big enough for two bites. But Jessie was always resourceful when it came to refreshments, and she soon had poured us two glasses of lemonade from a pitcher she found in the refrigerator, and had settled me at the kitchen table with the cardboard bakery box of extra cakes between us, when Mrs. Lockley reappeared, nodded to us silently, and went to the sink, where she began to wash green beans for dinner.

Jessie was right at her heels, carrying her glass in one hand, a crumbling, sticky tea cake in the other. "Mrs. Lockley," she begged, "tell Louise about the ghost."

Mrs. Lockley let the water rinse over the beans, and at first I didn't think she was going to answer Jessie. But Jessie was apparently used to Mrs. Lockley, and she persisted patiently. "I told Louise about the legend—but I want you to tell her, just like you told me."

Mrs. Lockley looked around at last and said, "I've already told you three times."

"But I want to hear it again," Jessie said. "I want Louise to hear it."

Mrs. Lockley let the water run over the beans a little longer while we waited. Then she put the beans in a bowl and carried them to the kitchen table, where she sat down with the bowl in her lap, snapping the beans into smaller pieces. She looked over at me, as though she were sizing me up and deciding if I were worth telling her story to. Jessie stood right at her elbow, licking frosting from her fingers and waiting calmly.

At last Mrs. Lockley said, "Well, the story goes back to when this house was built about sixty years ago by the Isherwood family. They traded sometimes at a little grocery store that my father owned over on Oak Street. Mr. Isherwood had gone to school with my father, right here in Westriver, and my father thought a lot of him. But he married a vain, selfish woman and my father didn't approve of her. They had one child, a daughter named Catherine, and my father used to say that Mrs. Isherwood raised her daughter in her own image—vain, spoiled, and willful. Young Catherine Isherwood was a beautiful girl for all her spoiled, silly ways. She never seemed to wear the same dress twice, and she had more beaux than any other girl in town. But my father used to say that her beauty would soon wither away with nothing to contemplate in her heart but herself."

Mrs. Lockley's hands clung motionlessly to the sides of the bowl as she forgot about breaking the beans. Jessie slid into a chair at the table beside me, and we both waited for the housekeeper to go on with her story. I think we had all forgotten more than the beans for dinner—or our lemonade and cakes. We had forgotten that other people sat on the

"Afterward, didn't he ever say whether he h
asked to break the engagement?"

"No, he would never talk about her. Maybe he d
cided that he had done all he could to be fair. The
again, maybe he never had given her any warning a
all. Nobody ever found out for sure. There were peo
ple in town who said they saw it all coming, tha
John Trevor had always been in love with Ellen but
he just got carried away for awhile by the prospects
of marrying into such a grand family as the Isherwoods."

"What was Ellen like?" I asked.

"A tiny, brown-haired, blue-eyed creature, meek as
a dove. And as sweet as Catherine Isherwood was
spoiled. Everybody liked Ellen, and gradually forgave John Trevor, as you might say, for running off
to marry her when he was engaged to Catherine. At
any rate, the young couple had quite a struggle for
many years. John Trevor had no special education to
speak of and his only prospect was the inheritance of
his father's upholstering shop. But John wasn't much
of a hand himself, and eventually he sold the business. After that he did a variety of jobs—carpentry,
selling furniture. They managed to get by and raised
two children. Then Ellen died a few years ago, and
he not long after."

"And tell what happened to Catherine Isherwood," Jessie prompted.

"Well, her mother took her abroad a few months
after John Trevor married Ellen Alton. They went

26

other side of the house, laughing and talking and
clinking ice in their glasses. And we forgot all the
years that had passed between this time and the time
Mrs. Lockley spoke of in her story.

"Whether my father was right or not," Mrs. Lockley continued, "Catherine Isherwood became engaged to a young man named John Trevor when she
was twenty. So I suppose she did have something to
contemplate in her heart besides herself. He was a
year or so older than she was. I was only about ten
years old then, but I remember him very well to this
day. His family did not quite come up to Mrs. Isherwood's expectations for Catherine, but Mr. Isherwood seemed to be satisfied. I remember he'd stop in
my father's store sometimes and he always spoke of
John Trevor as 'a fine lad.'"

"What was he like?" Jessie prompted. "John
Trevor, I mean."

"He was very charming and handsome, with dark
hair."

It made me think of Ritchie Allen. It made it easy
for me to picture Catherine Isherwood falling in love
with him.

"In the summertime, my older brother used to
make deliveries for Father, from the store," Mrs.
Lockley said, "and sometimes I'd ride along and he'd
let me hold the reins. It was quite a treat for me."

"The *reins*?" Jessie exclaimed, and Mrs. Lockley's
thin, dried-up-looking face broke into its first real
smile.

23

"Yes," she said importantly, "the reins. We delivered the groceries in a wagon pulled by Reuben, a big white horse."

"It sounds like fun," Jessie said wistfully.

"Well, it was work for my brother, but it was fun for me," Mrs. Lockley agreed. "Sometimes I'd run into one of the houses with him, carrying some bag or parcel that wasn't too heavy." She paused and looked around at the kitchen where we sat. "This room hasn't changed as much as you might think," she said. "Bobby—that was my brother—would bring in the boxes of groceries and put them on a table standing just about where this one is now.

"I remember once coming in with him and seeing Catherine Isherwood right over by that window, fussing because the girl who worked for them hadn't finished ironing a dress that Catherine wanted to wear. Then she stamped off, flouncing her skirts and hardly noticing us at all. Almost right away Mrs. Isherwood herself came steaming into the kitchen. The poor hired girl had just finished the dress then— fortunately for her, I suppose—and Mrs. Isherwood snatched it up and steamed away again.

"Then, as my brother and I were leaving with our wagon and old Reuben, we saw John Trevor walking up the street toward the house here, very gay and dapper looking, come to take Catherine for a stroll; and I thought that's what all the fuss was about, getting her ready for her beau. My brother Bobby and I were very impressed. We were always impressed with this house, with everything the Isherwood family did and everything they wore. Most of the town was. And besides all that," she concluded, "Mr. Isherwood was the mayor."

She waited to see that Jessie and I were also properly impressed by this. Her words came undramatically, simply spoken with a matter-of-factness, but we could hear the stamp of impatient heels across the floor, see the flouncing skirt and the angry toss of curls as Catherine went to tell her mother that her dress was not ready!

"Go on," Jessie urged, and Mrs. Lockley shook her head. "Ah," she said, "now the sad part comes. Suddenly, without any warning that anyone knew of, John Trevor and a girl named Ellen Alton, who lived nearby, ran off together and were married. It was quite a shock to everyone. Catherine was heartbroken—and unforgiving. She was heard on several occasions to say that she would pay them back, someday, somehow, in some way."

"But wasn't that a terrible thing for him to do?" I asked. "If they were engaged and all. How could he?"

"Men," Mrs. Lockley remarked serenely, "are capable of anything. I never trusted them much myself."

"But still," I said, "how could he do that without even telling her?"

Mrs. Lockley shrugged. "Maybe he did tell her. Maybe he wanted to break their engagement. Maybe he told her all about Ellen Alton. And maybe Catherine wouldn't let him break their engagement."

to Europe—I suppose to help Catherine mend her broken heart. I was here once before they left, and I saw Mrs. Isherwood talking to some friends in the hall there—" Mrs. Lockley pointed to the door that opened to the passageway leading to the front part of the house, closed now, separating us from the sound of voices in the living room. "She was standing very straight—a haughty woman, you'd say. When the visitors left she seemed to slump a little, and then she straightened and held her head up high and came stepping right out to the kitchen to see that nothing was missing from the grocery order. She was very pale and tired looking, I remember. Nothing pleased her. 'Why is the lettuce so poor?' she complained. 'Why does your father send me such miserable things?' My brother and I were frightened," Mrs. Lockley said, "and we ran away.

"It was only a day or so later that they left, Mrs. Isherwood and Catherine, for their trip. It was a quiet departure. Usually everything they did was written up on the front page of the paper. The town was so much smaller then and everything they did was news. We'd not have known they'd even gone, if Mr. Isherwood hadn't told my father in the store one afternoon.

"They were gone for two months. And on the homeward voyage their ship went down and they were lost at sea."

"You mean drowned?" I asked with a shiver.

"Everyone aboard," Mrs. Lockley said. "There

27

was not a single survivor."

The words settled in the quiet kitchen like strands of sea fog lying in the air, brushing our cheeks with a cold, wet touch. I glanced at Jessie, but she was watching Mrs. Lockley with a trancelike attention from her wide, unblinking eyes.

"Mr. Isherwood lived on here alone until he died an old man. He resigned his office as mayor and never went out in society again, nor was ever seen by anyone unless it was a glimpse of him walking in the garden. And then even that little bit of contact with the world seemed to be too much for him, and he had the wall built. Then hardly anyone ever saw him at all, except mischievous boys who would climb the wall sometimes or get up in the old apple tree that grows at the corner, outside the wall, and hang over the branches to see what they could see. It was one of the boys that first started the legend. He said there was someone walking with Mr. Isherwood in the garden one evening. He described Catherine Isherwood—although he was only a boy of ten or eleven and she had been dead since he was a baby. At first everyone had an explanation; the person, the woman, walking with Mr. Isherwood was a neighbor, a visiting relative, a servant—if she existed at all. But by and by over the years other, more reliable older people saw glimpses of someone in the garden with Mr. Isherwood—and one by one all the reasonable theories and explanations were proved empty. There *was* no explanation for what they saw or thought they saw. In her clothes, once so fine and now so long out of fashion that they were peculiar looking, Catherine Isherwood walked with her father in the garden where she had once sat hand in hand with her young lover, John Trevor.

"They said that she had returned home at last, to the place where she had been happy, to her father; and also, some people said, to somehow, someday, in some way pay back the wrong that had been done to her."

Jessie and I looked at each other over the bakery box of tea cakes. Outside the clouds had deepened over the sun, and there was an unnatural darkness to the sky for that time of day. Mrs. Lockley got up and switched on a ceiling light, carried her bowl of beans to the sink, and began to peel leaves from a fresh head of lettuce set there to drain. Her thin, quick fingers pulled at the delicate green leaves, and droplets of water flew out into the air.

"After Mr. Isherwood died, the house was left to his younger brother. But the brother had moved away from town years before and he didn't want the house. After it stood vacant a year or so, it was sold to a family by the name of Marriott. No one ever saw the ghost of the Isherwoods after Mr. Isherwood died. While the house was empty, children ran through the garden—when they dared—but they never saw her. The Marriott family lived here nearly ten years, then they sold the house to the Carew family. The Carews lived here three years. I worked for

29

them. Last year they sold the house to Jessie's folks."

"But the ghost is still here, isn't it?" Jessie whispered.

"Yes," Mrs. Lockley said. "The ghost is still here. It has nowhere else to go."

"But no one has ever seen it since Mr. Isherwood died?" I asked.

"No," Mrs. Lockley said. She stood very still a moment, and held her head erect.

"And you're not afraid of the ghost?" I said—registering far off in some corner of my mind that I really was sitting calmly in this strange kitchen talking about ghosts.

"No, I'm not afraid," she said, beginning to pull at the lettuce again. "It's not me she's after."

"But John Trevor and his wife are dead," I said.

Mrs. Lockley nodded. "That's so," she said. But that was all she would say. We watched a few minutes longer as she went about preparations for dinner, and then we were discovered by Aunt Vivian and Mother, who came out to the kitchen with the empty lemonade glasses and took us back to the front of the house with them to see Uncle Arthur, who had just come in. Don and Ritchie had gone for a walk, Mother said . . . and I wished they would hurry back so I could see Ritchie again. Father and Uncle Arthur went into the library after awhile, and when Don and Ritchie did come back, hands in pockets, looking up to see the first drops of rain that seemed surely about to come at any moment from the darkened sky, I pretended to be very busy fooling around at the piano with Jessie and wouldn't even look up at them when they came in.

"This is Jessie," I heard someone say. "Jessie, this is Donald's friend, Ritchie Allen."

And I heard Jessie say, "Hi," and I heard Ritchie say, "Hi, Jessie," and I pretended I could feel his eyes burning holes in my back, but I wouldn't turn around. Such, at fifteen, was my approach to romance.

Later that evening, while we were all sitting around the table in the dining room finishing the ice cream with chocolate syrup that Mrs. Lockley had fixed for dessert, I remembered the cat I had seen in the garden.

"Where is the cat?" I asked, and Uncle Arthur said, "What cat?"

"The cat," I repeated. "I saw it in the garden this afternoon. The black cat."

"There's no cat here," Aunt Vivian said, frowning a little.

"But I saw it from the window upstairs," I said. "It was sitting on the flagstones. A big black cat."

Mrs. Lockley came from the kitchen with a fresh server of coffee, and Aunt Vivian said, "It was probably some stray that came in through the gate. Mrs. Lockley, have you seen a cat around here?"

Mrs. Lockley hesitated a moment, then she said, "No, Mrs. Ellison, I haven't. There hasn't been a cat in this house for nearly fifty years—not since Catherine Isherwood lived here. She had a black cat she was very fond of. She took it with her when she went away, and it was drowned with her at sea."

Aunt Vivian opened her mouth as though she were going to say something, and then she closed it again, thinking better of what she'd meant to say. "Thank you, Mrs. Lockley," she said evenly, and Mrs. Lockley went back through the passageway toward the kitchen, quickly lost in the gloomy shadows that filled the passage.

"Goodness," Aunt Vivian exclaimed, jumping up suddenly, "let's have some lights on around here." And before anyone could get up to help, she had switched on the light in the passageway, and an extra light at the side of the dining room.

"There," she said, as the passageway sprang into view, clean and ordinary looking, empty except for a small table with a plant in a brass pot. "That's better."

The kitchen door was swinging where Mrs. Lockley had gone through, and there was reassurance in the familiar sound of dishes clinking and water running in the sink.

CHAPTER THREE

MY COUSIN MARCELLA came the next morning while
we were all at church. Aunt Sybil had telephoned
just as we were getting ready for bed the night before to say that Marcella would be taking an early
train from Albany in the morning. It did not come to
Westriver, but to a nearby town called Garland, and
Uncle Arthur, freshly shaved and jovial, went off to
meet the train while the rest of us were still sprinkled
about the house in our various rooms getting ready
for church. It had not rained after all, but the sky
remained overcast and the air was cool that Sunday
morning. When we came back from church at
twelve, Marcella was sitting in the living room looking slim and glamorous with her yellowy hair done
up in a bun and about sixteen bracelets rattling on
her arms.

Sunday was Mrs. Lockley's day off, and Uncle Arthur had fixed Marcella a dish of ice cream to eat.
She was just finishing, and she set her dish on the
table and got up to receive Aunt Vivian's outstretched arms and cries of delight that she had
come. "Marcella, darling, how wonderful to see
you!"

As Aunt Vivian gave her a good hug, Marcella smiled around at everyone, but I noticed that her eyes flickered over us rather hastily and came to rest on Ritchie Allen. I suppose she had heard that he would be here. (I could just hear Aunt Sybil saying, *Aunt Vivian wants you to come for a visit; Aunt Winifred and Uncle Charles will be there with Don and Louise and Don's handsome friend—you remember, the young man we met at Christmas, Marcella*. And I could hear Marcella saying, *Oh, yes, I believe I do remember him. Maybe I will visit dear Aunt Vivian awhile*.)

And here she was.

Ritchie had been teasing me about something as we came through the house, but now he forgot me entirely, and spent the rest of the day hovering over Marcella. It was just like the Christmas holiday all over again.

The day continued cloudy and damp and cool. Rain was surely coming today, everyone said. Marcella soon changed from her traveling clothes into a pink striped cotton dress and a pair of straw sandals. She put a band of pink ribbon around her bun of hair and managed to look even more beautiful than ever and to be the center of attention all through dinner. Aunt Vivian wanted to know how Aunt Sybil was, and Uncle Arthur wanted to know how the train ride was—and Jessie wanted to hear about the modeling school. So did I, but I wouldn't lower myself to ask Marcella. I sipped my iced tea and tried to look bored whenever Ritchie glanced in my direction, so that he would think modeling schools were of no interest to someone as sophisticated as I already was. This was not particularly effective, because he did not glance in my direction very much—but Mother did ask me once if I was feeling all right.

With Mrs. Lockley gone for the day, her story seemed to fade somewhat from the reality I had felt the afternoon before . . . until midway through dinner when I felt myself turning warily around in my chair almost involuntarily to stare into the empty passageway where I was sure someone had been standing watching us at the table. But there was no one there, and Mother asked again if anything was wrong with me.

"No," I answered, seeing Jessie's eyes upon me, round and solemn—and hearing, as though somewhere far off, Marcella's laughter and my brother Don saying, ". . . don't tell me you're on another diet? What happened to the bananas and skimmed milk . . ." And a faint rumbling of thunder nearby made me notice how dark the day had grown again. Like yesterday when we were listening to Mrs. Lockley's story in the kitchen, only even darker.

Mother smoothed back her hair and gave my arm a pat. She turned her attention to something Daddy was saying. I watched her turning her diamond rings, which she did unconsciously sometimes, and I noticed her lovely, slender, perfectly manicured fingers with oval nails and delicate moons, tinted with colorless polish and scented with a perfumed hand cream that Mother carried with her wherever she went. As I watched her hands against the white of the cloth, it seemed as though something like a shadow fell across them for an instant—but it was only the darkening of the sky and the fading of light that came through the dining-room window upon the table.

It was during the afternoon, when Jessie, Marcella, Don, and Ritchie and I were in the library—our parents were sitting talking in the living room across the hall—that the rain started at last. The first few large spattery drops hit the terrace doors and clung heavily against the glass. Glowing lamps hardly seemed to touch the gloom that grew in the corners, sending dark shadows upward to the ceiling in grotesque, out-of-shape sizes. A wind, beginning through the trees in the garden, twisted leaves down to the ground, and branches of a thorny bush by the terrace scraped against the edge of the doors with each tug of the wind, like witches' fingers scratching at the glass.

Jessie sat on the arm of Marcella's chair and told her about the ghost of Catherine Isherwood, just the way Mrs. Lockley had told us. Don and Ritchie sat at the card table with Uncle Arthur's chess set between them, and before long they were listening, too.

I sat back, feeling at an advantage because I had heard the story. I tilted my chin up importantly, resting my head back against the high leather chair, my legs curled under me and my full print skirt spread out around me like some elegant old-

fashioned dress. . . . *Once at Christmastime I had*
been sitting like that, all curled up and surrounded
by skirts, and Ritchie had said, "Little Miss Muffet
sits on her tuffet," and kissed me as he held a piece of
mistletoe over my head . . .

Yet now, despite my sense of importance, Marcella
managed to be the center of attention again. She sat
with her legs crossed, one dainty straw sandal now
and then tapping the air. Hands clasped under her
chin, she listened to Jessie with an amused expression
on her face. "Oh, Jessie," she broke in a time or two,
"you don't really *believe* all this!"

"I do too!" Jessie answered firmly each time. And
at last, to back her up, I told Marcella about seeing
the black cat sitting on the terrace by the iron bench.

Marcella didn't know what to say to that, and then
Ritchie got up in his lazy, teasing, good-natured way,
and came over toward us. He lounged against the
edge of Uncle Arthur's desk, arms crossed, one leg
slightly forward for balance.

"If you see any ghosts around here, I'll protect you,
Marcella," he said, teasing, but smiling at her as
though they had some special secret between them. I
felt left out, absolutely forlorn. It was awful to see
them smiling at each other. Miss Muffet and the
mistletoe at Christmastime seemed a million years
away now; I was sure that Ritchie Allen had forgotten I existed on the earth. As they smiled at each
other, I thought they had forgotten Jessie and her
story, too, but despite whatever silent communica-

37

tion they exchanged with their smiles, they were still listening—for in a moment Marcella interrupted again.

"Oh, Jessie, how *can* you *believe* that?"

And then Ritchie said, "How can *you* doubt it, Marcella?" As we looked at him, his eyes traveled over the room; he shrugged and gestured to the shadowy corners, the rainy, dark garden, and the scratch of the bush against the door. "Doesn't it seem even a little spooky to you?" He winked at Jessie, and then looked at Marcella, waiting to see what she would say.

Jessie wasn't sure whether Ritchie was taking her side or not. She got up and began fiddling with a box of checkers on the desk. Marcella shrugged and looked around. Then she said, "I guess you're right, Ritchie. It is kind of, well, I guess spooky is the right word. It's so gloomy and dreary today."

"Not dreary—eerie," Ritchie corrected, with a finger pointed wisely into the air.

Don tilted back in his chair by the card table and surprised us all by saying: "I agree with Jessie. There is something odd about this house." His face was serious; his eyes, light grayish-green like mine, looked unusually dark and thoughtful. "It gives me the creeps."

We were all silent for a few moments. It seemed somehow disrespectful to Aunt Vivian and Uncle Arthur—who were always so good to all of us—to speak of their house that way; only the fact that

Jessie herself felt the same way about the house saved us from even guiltier feelings. Marcella fingered a ruffle on her skirt, as we all avoided meeting each other's eyes. When she did look up, she looked at Ritchie, to see what he might have to say. I felt a depressing kinship to Catherine Isherwood, who had lived in this house so many years before and been in love with a dark, handsome man who ran off with another girl. I thought I knew how she must have felt.

Ritchie didn't say anything for a moment. He looked over his shoulder at Cousin Jessie, who, having told her story and started us all feeling ghosts in the room, had withdrawn to the swivel chair behind the desk. She was calmly setting red checkers in one row and black checkers in another at opposite ends of the board, though no one yet had agreed to play with her.

Then, still teasing, Ritchie looked from Jessie at the desk to Don, tilted back in his chair by the chess set. "Checkers? Chess?" Ritchie said, shaking his head in mock surprise. "This place seems more suitable to a game of Spiders and Spooks." His voice sank melodramatically. "You know, advance to the ghoul's grave; go back two spaces and take a card from the dead man's eye—that's what the witches and ghosts play, and the trolls who live under the bridges in dank woods, and all those creepy, crawly, horrible things."

Marcella started and shivered nervously. "Ritchie,

stop," she said, and Jessie cried at her, "You're scared!"

"I am *not!*" Marcella got up and twitched over to the desk, looking around at us defiantly. "Scared?" she said scornfully. "Of all this nonsense and these silly stories?"

"You are *too* scared," Jessie insisted determinedly, tilting up her chin and staring at Marcella boldly.

"If this is really a haunted house, why did your mother and father buy it?" Marcella demanded.

"It wasn't spooky when we first came," Jessie said.

"Well, why is it suddenly spooky *now?*"

"I don't know," Jessie answered. "No one knows."

"No one knows," Marcella mimicked lightly. "Oh, Jessie, nobody but a *child* would believe that story."

Jessie stared back fiercely, but Marcella only tossed her head, and then turned and switched on the radio on a table by the terrace doors. She fiddled with the dials until she found some music, and she held out her arms to Ritchie.

"Dance with me, Ritchie," she invited.

I watched helplessly as he put his arms around her and they began to dance. She gave Jessie one last impudent look before closing her eyes and snuggling against Ritchie's shoulder. She trailed one hand limply, as though she were too fragile to hold it up properly.

Don watched them a little, and then, still tilted back in the chair, he turned his attention to the gray, wet garden, watching the falling rain thoughtfully. Jessie bent her head so low over the checkerboard that her hair fell forward, hiding her face and touching the checkers. After a minute she got up and came over and sat down on the arm of my chair.

Softly she said to me, "Lets us do something to show Marcella that this house is really haunted."

Slowly I dragged my eyes away from watching Ritchie and Marcella dance. Jessie was waiting for an answer, leaning close toward me, her eyes shining.

"Like what?" I asked vaguely.

"I'll think of something." Her expression as Marcella and Ritchie danced by was blank, innocent, and under her breath she continued, "Will you help me, Louise?" Her words were more ominous by being half-whispered from the innocent face. She smiled angelically across the room at Marcella.

Marcella smiled back at us, and I realized that I had been smiling too; then she forgot us and said something to Ritchie that we could not hear over the radio music, just as what Jessie and I said softly to each other could not be heard by them. I felt the smile trembling on my face as I watched them dancing and talking softly to each other.

"All right, I'll help you," I said, and Jessie slid off the arm of my chair and went nonchalantly back to the desk, where she began aimlessly pushing checkers from square to square, humming to herself.

In the garden, a stronger wind and faster-falling rain blew wet leaves against the glass French doors,

41

and the winged horses were lit by faint flickers of lightning. I got up and went to stand by the doors, and the others came and stood beside me, as though we were all somehow drawn to the windows by some force that we could not understand. The sky had a dreadful, deep, soft, dark look to it, as if it were slowly coming down upon us like a closed, airless bag in which we would be caught, blind and suffocating.

I thought I saw something move across an open stretch of lawn at the side.

"There's the cat again!" I cried.

For an instant the yellow eyes glowed at me and then the black shape disappeared into the shrubbery along the wall.

Marcella did not look as scornful as she had before. She seemed subdued by the rainy garden and queer sky, but she said: "Silly, cats don't go out in the rain."

"No, I suppose they don't," I said slowly, not taking my eyes from the spot where the black cat had disappeared, "not *real* cats, anyway."

"Oh, for goodness' sake!" Marcella said; but then everything was silent, and somewhere in the house we heard a door close and click softly, tightly into place.

"What was that?" Jessie asked, looking around at us accusingly.

Marcella and Ritchie looked at each other and over at me. Don shook his head and shrugged, and then we were all very quiet, but there was nothing more to hear.

I can pick out that rainy Sunday afternoon by itself from all the memories of days that have gone before and since; I can almost pick it up and hold it and look at it and see us standing by the terrace doors—like figures in one of those hollow sugar eggs children have at Easter . . . or imprisoned in a glass paperweight in which rain is falling instead of snow.

But quiet as we were, there was nothing more to hear.

We stood looking out at the sky coming down on us and the strange, large drops clinging to the glass of the French doors.

CHAPTER FOUR

THAT NIGHT a thick fog covered the house and the garden, the street beyond the wall, the town. Uncle Arthur and Daddy had driven out to get some things for Aunt Vivian at a little dairy store that she knew was open on Sunday nights, and they came back inching slowly along, their headlights glowing at us through the haze as they swung into the drive.

Everyone went to bed early, and Jessie and I put on our pajamas and talked and ate cookies and cold-bloodedly planned what we would do to scare Marcella. We had no difficulty keeping awake until we were sure that everyone else in the house was sleeping. But we were impatient. A silence settled down as thickly as the fog, and we opened Jessie's door several times and listened to the absolute stillness of midnight.

Jessie had brought a book up from the library with her, smuggled under her sweater. It was called only *Ghost Tales*, but the black cover decorated with a single groping white hand that seemed to glow with light from some pit of horrors sent a tingle up my back just to look at it. We decided to put the book at Marcella's door.

"What I'd *really* like to do is put something wet and cold in her bed," Jessie said regretfully. "But I guess it's too late for that—she's already in her room."

"We couldn't do that anyway," I said. "She'd probably scare the whole house with her screaming."

So we ate our cookies and waited for one o'clock, which we felt would be a safe time; and I wonder now how we could have been so mean. I still blush guiltily to think that however innocently wicked my cousin Jessie was about her plans, I was three years older—old enough to know better! But I was jealous because Marcella was so pretty and had danced with Ritchie Allen, and Jessie's suggestion gave me a chance to do something about it.

"What we really need is some great big horrible-looking dead bug to put right on top of the book," Jessie said thoughtfully.

"Well, you can't get one now," I said, flinching at the thought. Jessie was actually looking toward the windows as if, with a little encouragement from me, she might run out into the fog and kill a bug.

She shrugged and admitted, "No, I suppose I can't get one now. Maybe if I get up early enough in the morning I can find something and push it into her room under the door or something."

She was silent a moment, and then added regretfully, "If I'd only thought of it sooner. There must be lots of bugs in the garden."

"Well, you can't get one now," I reminded her

45

again, as she once more began looking toward the window speculatively.

"I wouldn't go out there now anyway," she said after a moment.

We seemed to agree that nobody in the world would have gone out on that wet, foggy night into the tangling garden—past the terrace and the iron bench, past the stone horses and the birdbath and the flowerbeds, out to the bushes and vines and undergrowth that grew from the wall inward as if the stalks and crooked branches would in time overtake everything and grow upon the very walls of the house itself.

At last we decided it was late enough for us to pursue our plan, and we took a sheet from Jessie's bed and draped it over her, laying it so that it hung at her sides and in front of her and swept the floor behind her. We had to fuss with it until she could see through a fold, since we didn't dare cut the sheet. Holding our breaths, feeling our way in the darkness, we went into the corridor and separated. I went back along the hall, carrying the book of ghost tales.

Next to Jessie's room was a large linen closet, then a bathroom, and opposite it, at the end of the hall, was Marcella's room, a small room that was probably supposed to be a servant's room, but wasn't used because Mrs. Lockley didn't live at the house. Aunt Vivian used it as a sewing room, and a folding bed had been set up in there for Marcella. It was only a step or two from this room across the hall and around the corner to the back stairway, which led down to the passageway by the kitchen.

As my eyes grew accustomed to the darkness, I could see the faint outlines of the hallway, doors, and the window at the end of the hall by the backstairs. From the front hall downstairs, where a nightlight always burned, came a soft bluish glow. Jessie went to the big front stairway and stood there silhouetted by the dim light from below, a huge, shapeless form, nothing more identifiable than a dark outline that moved without sound.

I put the book by Marcella's door, and knocked softly. Then I ran at once to the backstairs around the corner and stayed out of sight.

Marcella must have been awake, for almost at once I heard the door open. Unable to resist the temptation to peek, I saw her standing in her doorway. Light from a small lamp she had turned on spilled out into the hallway across the carpet and upon the black and hideous cover of *Ghost Tales*. From the front end of the hall, Jessie was walking slowly but steadily toward Marcella. She lifted her arms out from her sides so that the sheet looked like some ghostly floating robe, and great shadows chased upward along the walls to the ceiling.

I pressed back again into my hiding place on the top step of the back stairway, and then I heard a noise behind me—a soft noise like a sigh or a whisper or a drawn breath, nothing more—and whirling in fright, I saw in the darkness, barely broken by the faint light from the hall, a shadow on the stairs, something drawn back and pressed close against the wall to hide, just as I was doing. I was too frightened to scream or move, and in the blackness, five or six steps below me, whatever, whoever it was made no move either; but I knew something was there, watching me from the darkness.

Then Marcella slammed her door, abruptly shattering the silence. The faint light cast by her lamp was gone. The stairs below me were plunged into total darkness, and there was a sound of movement I cannot exactly describe. It was not the sound of footsteps or the rustle of clothes, or even the creaking of boards on the stairs; it was nothing as familiar and definite as that; but it *was* the sound of something going away from me down the stairs. Then the sound was over, and I knew if every light in the house blazed on suddenly, I would see only an empty stairway below me.

I stayed where I was, trembling and waiting. But Marcella did not open her door again, and after a minute or so I heard Jessie tiptoeing along toward me, trailing her sheet, whispering, "Louise, where are you?" There was such a welcomeness to this familiar and understandable sound, and I came cautiously from my place at the corner.

"Come on," Jessie hissed. "She's not coming out again."

We tiptoed softly past Marcella's door to Jessie's room, where we sat in the dark in case Marcella should look out into the hall again and see a light under our door.

"We really scared her," Jessie whispered with glee, struggling out from under the layers of bedsheet. "But she didn't touch the book. We'll think of something scarier to do tomorrow night."

"Oh, no," I said. "We can't do anything else, Jessie. There was something on the stairs, where I was standing."

"What was it?" Jessie drew close to me in the darkness. I could imagine the intensity of her thin little-girl face, her hair falling forward like a dark curtain across her cheeks.

"I don't know what, exactly," I said. "Something was there, in the shadows. Only it was like a shadow itself, big and dark—and it moved."

"It *did*?" Jessie's voice quivered with awe and fright and excitement. "Oh, Louise, I told you the story was true. Mrs. Lockley *said* the ghost was here. She's right, isn't she, Louise? The ghost *is* here."

"Oh, Jessie, I don't know I-I-I just know we mustn't scare Marcella anymore. Let's——" I stopped suddenly.

"Let's what?" Jessie asked.

I was going to say let's go back and take the book away. It was still lying in the hall by Marcella's door. But I didn't want to go back out into that hall again, into that darkness.

"Never mind," I said.

We got under the covers and somehow, surprisingly, were able to fall asleep eventually. When I woke in the morning, the sheet was heaped up on the floor where Jessie had left it. She was dressed and gone, and when I went down the hall to the bathroom to wash my face and brush my teeth I saw what she had been up to so early: on the cover of *Ghost Tales*—still lying on the floor by Marcella's closed door—was a large dead black garden beetle, a little squashed, but all the more horrible for that, flat and glistening, with its legs sprawled across the white of the ghostly hand.

CHAPTER FIVE

"Oh, it's not going to be *another* dark rainy day!" Aunt Vivian said, standing by the dining-room windows and peering past the curtain she had drawn aside. "It's such a shame. Ever since you've come it's been cold and rainy."

Daddy laughed. "Maybe we should go home and take our rain clouds with us," he said. He was sitting with Mother and Uncle Arthur at one end of the dining-room table.

Mother passed the sugar to me and I sprinkled some on a bowl of cereal and began to eat, wondering where Jessie had gone to and what I was ever going to do when Marcella came downstairs.

"It just seems a shame." Aunt Vivian sighed and sank into a chair at the table, waving her hand to decline Uncle Arthur's offer to pour her another cup of coffee. "You'll only be here a week, and the house is so much—well, so much nicer when it's not so gloomy and rainy."

"I think this kind of weather makes houses seem even nicer and cozier," Mother said, to cheer up Aunt Vivian.

"You know, it's odd, but this house just isn't like

51

that," Aunt Vivian said reflectively. "Now that I think back, it never has been 'cozy' on dark days; it just seems bigger than usual, sort of echoey—and sort of gloomy." Aunt Vivian remembered me and added hastily, "But I don't mean scary, like Jessie says; it's just at its best on bright, sunny days."

"Ummm." Mother nodded and thought this over to herself, stirring her coffee.

"It's like some people, I guess," Aunt Vivian went on conversationally. "Some people don't mind dark, cloudy, rainy days, but other people can't *stand* them. Don't you remember Uncle Wilton?" she said to Mother. "Uncle Wilton couldn't do anything on rainy days—he admitted it. He said he felt like he was hollow inside when the sun wasn't shining. He couldn't think about anything except how gloomy and dark it was; it was like an obsession."

"Yes, I do sort of remember that," Mother answered, sifting back through her memories to her childhood and Uncle Wilton feeling hollow inside when the sun wasn't shining.

"Uncle Wilton would have hollowed out altogether here, I'm afraid," Uncle Arthur said cheerfully. He was a big, hearty man, and everything he said came out in a deep, hearty voice. His blue eyes twinkled merrily at Aunt Vivian.

"Arthur," Aunt Vivian scolded. "You're beginning to sound like Jessie. It will probably be sunny by afternoon."

"I'm sure it will." Uncle Arthur laughed and gave

me a broad wink. Then he said, "What do you think of our house, young lady?"

I thought about that dreadful shadow on the stairway, but I couldn't say anything. I certainly couldn't tell what Jessie and I were doing prowling around in the hallway at one o'clock in the morning.

"I think it's very nice," I answered politely. I even managed to give Uncle Arthur a faint smile.

Jessie appeared, much to my relief, before Marcella. She came from the kitchen carrying a large bowl of strawberries that Mrs. Lockley had just cleaned and sugared for us, and she seemed very bright and chatty and innocent-looking in her little blue sundress and blue hairbow, carrying her bowl of strawberries. She didn't look as though she had been creeping around in a sheet in the middle of the night—or had been out at sunup to kill a beetle in the garden. Her hair was brushed back neatly, and only by a surreptitious little smile did she acknowledge to me that she was really the same Jessie.

But we both felt pangs of uncertainty when we heard Marcella coming down the stairs and through the hall to the dining room. Jessie darted a glance at me, and then we lowered our eyes over our dishes of strawberries and pretended to be busy eating.

Marcella had evidently decided to say nothing of what happened the night before, for she sat down at the table—looking very fresh and shining, with all her makeup on from lipstick to mascara—and proceeded to eat her breakfast quite calmly. (Later we discovered that she had put *Ghost Tales* and the dead beetle in Jessie's room, with a little note that said, *Thanks. I've already read this book.* That made me feel foolish and childish.)

"Did you sleep well, dear?" Aunt Vivian asked Marcella. Aunt Vivian had not been entirely satisfied with the folding bed that had been put up for Marcella, and she seemed to doubt that anyone could really get a good night's rest upon it.

"Yes, I slept just fine," Marcella replied sweetly, and included everyone at the table in her smile—particularly, I thought, Jessie and me. She was pretty, I admitted to myself with a forlorn feeling; it wasn't just going to modeling school and putting on airs that made her attractive. She had lovely gray eyes and delicate features and soft yellow hair and the most beautiful clear skin ... *"Do you use Lovely-Lovely Soap?"* ... *"Yes, indeed I do and you should too!"* ... Words from a familiar television commercial jingled through my mind.

Just then Don stuck his head in from the hall and said, "Hey, anybody want to go for a ride uptown?" Jessie and Marcella and I all said Yes and went trooping after him in a flurry of getting our purses and sweaters and combing our hair one more time.

Uncle Arthur came after us and insisted that we take his car because it was a convertible and we could ride along with the top down. He gave the keys to Don, who drove the car around from the garage to the front of the house—and somehow I found myself in the front seat between Don and Ritchie. Ritchie had his arm along the back of the seat behind me, and I could almost pretend that he had it around my shoulders. I felt exhilarated and happy, and I didn't care how many ghosts and dark shadows we left behind in that strange house and that strange garden. I wanted to ride along in that car forever with my brother Don on one side, driving, and Ritchie Allen on the other side, with his arm across the back of the seat. The car was a deep red with red leather upholstery and whitewall tires. It was a powerful car, shined to a high gloss and bright with chrome. In the backseat, Marcella tied a scarf on her head and put on sunglasses (although there was no sun), and Jessie let her dark hair whip around her face, shaking it out like a mane behind her and laughing as she felt it blow.

But we didn't go uptown right away. Don was too eager to drive Uncle Arthur's convertible on an open stretch of road before he had to ease along side streets and poke through traffic. We went out of town and sped along into the country, watching pastures and farmhouses and clumps of woods go by, raising up clouds of brown birds that had settled onto the highway as if it were theirs.

At one place, some children hanging on a gate waved to us as we zoomed by, and I suppose watched after us until we were too far away to see anymore.

Then Don and Ritchie changed places, and Ritchie

drove. We headed back toward town, flashing over the smooth surface of the highway as though we could go on forever riding into the wind and never have to stop and do ordinary things again.

Gradually the farmhouses and pastures fell behind us, and we came to the outskirts of town; first a few houses along the roadway and then the quiet residential streets, and at last the business section. Parking meters lined the curbs and the lights flashed around the movie theater marquee for the afternoon show.

"Let's have lunch at the Malt House," Jessie suggested pointing to a place along the street. "We can call Mother; she won't mind."

"I'm starving," Marcella said agreeably, sitting forward on the edge of the seat, and perking up to look at the clothes in the shopwindows as we went by. "Oh, there's a wonderful movie playing. Why don't we all go tonight?"

Ritchie parked, and we were starting to get out when a girl walking along the street called to Jessie.

"Hi, Audrey," Jessie answered, and the girl came over to the car, looking at us curiously. She was a tall girl with sleek almost-black hair and big dark eyes. She was about eighteen, and she looked at Ritchie and Don with a cool, poised expression. In one hand she carried a large straw handbag, and in the other arm she had a few small packages balanced on a large cardboard dress box from *Ann's Dress Shoppe,* which was just a short distance down the street.

Jessie introduced us all and said, "This is Audrey Dickenson; she lives next door."

For the first time I was struck by the fact that at Uncle Arthur and Aunt Vivian's house, with its walled garden and high trees, I had never once thought of anyone "living next door." The house seemed so alone somehow, apart from things, cut off and isolated. Now I realized that somewhere on the side opposite the garden and the street corner, there was not only a house-next-door, but ordinary, every-day people, just like we had at home in the house next door to us.

"Audrey's getting ready for college," Jessie said.

Audrey shrugged under the weight of her bundles. "I think I'm just about through getting ready after today," she said. "At least, my money's through!"

Ritchie was still sitting behind the wheel, but Don had been standing on the sidewalk putting money in the parking meter, and he quickly reached over and scooped up Audrey's packages into his arms, where they rested lightly, no burden for him at all.

"There," he said, leaning toward her and smiling his special smile-for-girls. "Isn't that better?"

"Oh, much better," Audrey said, smiling back at

him with an expression that said she knew he smiled that way at all the girls; in fact, it was a sort of smile-for-boys, and I could see they were going to get along great together.

"Have lunch with us," Jessie invited, getting out of the backseat and holding the door for Marcella. Marcella took off her scarf and fluffed out her hair with her fingers.

Audrey hesitated. "Oh, I don't know——" she said slowly.

Immediately my brother Don said, "Sure, that's a swell idea. Any friend of Jessie's is a friend of ours, I always say." And before Audrey had time to make up her mind one way or the other, he had his arm securely through hers and was leading her off down the street. Jessie ran after them to tell Don he was going in the wrong direction. Marcella, Ritchie, and I closed the car doors and led the way to the Malt House.

Don made quite a hit with Audrey, and before we had finished our sandwiches and cokes she had agreed to go with us to the movies that night—or, to go with Don would be more accurate. She laughed and twisted the paper wrapper from her straw into a curlicue and twitched it on the tabletop as she talked, and I wondered what beautiful things for college she had in the packages on the chair beside her. Being fifteen began to seem younger and younger, and no place quite so ignominious as second year, high school.

"What's the matter, Little Miss Muffet?" Ritchie asked, leaning across the table toward me when, for the moment, everybody else was busy talking together.

"Nothing. Why?" I'm sure I looked startled that he had called me that, and I wondered in that instant if he had somehow, someway, read my thoughts.

He leaned back and looked at me without saying anything for a moment, and then he leaned toward me again and—tweaked my nose! I felt overcome with disappointment and helpless rage. How did he dare to do that—something one did to *children*. I felt humiliated and close to tears.

He couldn't possibly have known how hurt I was by that gesture, and almost right away he turned to laugh at something funny Jessie said.

I gulped down my hurt feelings and unshed tears, and tried to look interested as Audrey Dickenson explained to my brother that she had one more errand to do before she could go home, and Don agreed to go along and help her carry her packages.

And I wouldn't look at Ritchie Allen again.

Somehow the memory of the wonderful morning ride was ruined, and when we went back to the car I deliberately got into the backseat with Jessie and let Marcella and Ritchie sit together in the front seat. Don strolled away with Audrey, carrying her packages. They were going to drive home in her car, and we all waved good-bye to each other as Ritchie pulled away from the curb. Marcella curled up on the front seat beside him and rested her head back against the smooth new leather. I thought briefly about Don and Audrey driving home in her car, and it seemed yet another relentless reminder of all that separated fifteen from older, more glamorous ages. I wouldn't even be old enough for a learner's permit for another year.

I thought about what I would wear that night when we all went to the movies, and when we got home and Jessie went to take a bath, I got out all the dresses I had brought for the week (only three and not even my very best one). I laid them out on the bed and one by one held them up in front of me as I stood by the mirror and tried to think of something different and sophisticated I could do with my hair to make me look older . . . and I wondered if perhaps Catherine Isherwood might not have stood in that very room sometimes, so many years ago, studying her reflection in a mirror and trying to decide what to wear to go dancing or out walking with John Trevor . . .

"I like that dress best," Marcella said from the

doorway, and then she came in and sat on the edge of the bed by the dresses and put her head to one side to consider them.

"I wish I could do something different with my hair," I said, although, of course, I couldn't add, *to make Ritchie Allen forget you and notice me.*

Marcella said, "Well, let me see," and she began to push my hair back from my face this way and that, trying it in different ways.

My hair is yellow, almost the same color as hers, and I wore it then shoulder length, parted on the side and curled under slightly in a loose pageboy. Bangs fell over my forehead almost to my eyes.

"I like your hair the way it is," Marcella said, "but if you want a change, try pulling it back behind your ears and putting a clip on the side—right here." She stuck a hairpin in place to hold the hair where she wanted it for a minute.

"There, do you like that?" She stood back and let me study my reflection. I did look older, more sophisticated with my hair back and the hairpin catching the side of it where the part made it fullest.

"Yes, I guess so——" I said slowly, turning this way and that with growing satisfaction.

"Only you can't just wear a hairpin," Marcella said, and went off to her room and came back with a wide silver hair clip that she said I could borrow.

"Thank you," I said, feeling contrite because she was being so nice and helpful.

"Oh, that's all right," she said. She gave my hair a

last little pat into place. "You really look very sweet."

She meant it to be complimentary, I know, but after she had gone I couldn't help wishing she had said that I looked gorgeous or stunning, something more exciting than "sweet."

At last I hung the dresses back in the closet, except for the dark blue dress with the white embroidered flowers, which I decided made me look the oldest. I hung that one on the closet door, and got out my pearls and my white shoes. Jessie came back from her bath and decided she wouldn't go to the movie after all because she wanted to make something with a tile set she had. A tray, she thought. *Why* she decided to do it on that particular night, I couldn't understand—but she was, after all, only twelve and she just decided that she wanted to make a tray with the tile set, and nothing could dissuade her.

I put on the blue dress and the white pumps anyway, and wore them to dinner; but I began to feel more and more like an extra girl. Aunt Vivian had invited Audrey to come for dinner when she heard that Audrey was going to the show with us, and she arrived in a pale green dress that made her black hair look even shinier and blacker than usual. Marcella wore a black sheath dress and pearls; she looked a lot older than sixteen, I thought, and I wondered how she had talked her mother into letting her buy a black sheath dress. Ritchie and Marcella and Don and Audrey seemed so nicely paired off together. When I saw the four of them standing in the hall getting ready to go, I felt more and more out of place, and I went into the library and sat down at the table where Jessie had spread out her tiles and tube of cement and folded, crinkly papers with directions for making candy dishes and trivets and wall decorations from the tiny mosaic tiles.

No one seemed bowled over by surprise when I said—quite casually—that I thought I'd stay home and help Jessie, and I saw how easily they could shift me from group to group, being at the in-between age I was; and I pretended to be very interested in reading instructions about the tiles as I heard the car drive off outside. But I wasn't really reading. I wished that I were one age or the other—if I couldn't be seventeen or eighteen, grown-up and old enough to drive a car and go to college and have Ritchie Allen notice me (and *not* tweak my nose!), then I'd rather be twelve like Jessie and not even care about anything except catching beetles in the garden and making a tray out of colored tiles.

CHAPTER SIX

Tuesday was the day Aunt Vivian had planned for the picnic at the river. It was cloudy but warmer, and according to the weather reports the day was not supposed to be rainy.

The kitchen lights were on early in the morning, as Aunt Vivian and Mother puttered around with Mrs. Lockley, getting breakfast and packing the picnic baskets at the same time. There were hard-boiled eggs and fried chicken, sandwiches and chocolate cake and a basket of fruit. There seemed to be nothing else in the kitchen except picnic lunch—but then, if you looked closely, you could see there was also a skillet for breakfast eggs and a plate of cinnamon toast and a row of glasses filled with orange juice. When Jessie and I came to the kitchen door, Mother put the tray of juice glasses in my hands and said, "Now you two get out from underfoot. Here, take this into the dining room."

Jessie followed me, carrying the cinnamon toast. Don and Ritchie were sitting at the table with Uncle Arthur and Daddy, and Marcella came down a moment later.

"Good," Aunt Vivian said, hurrying in from the

kitchen to get extra saltcellars from the dining-room buffet. "Everybody's up. We'll get a nice early start."

Every summer that I could remember when we had come to visit Aunt Vivian and Uncle Arthur and Jessie, we had spent one whole day at the river having a picnic. Aunt Vivian threw herself into the preparations for it with a vigorous delight, although just to look at her you'd certainly say she was not the type to sit on a grassy riverbank among the ants, eating a piece of fried chicken. And even Mother always surprised me as she bustled around helping Aunt Vivian—though Mother tended to lean heavily toward remembering things like blankets and straw hats because she hated to sit on bare ground and she freckled easily. Therefore she thought that everyone else ought to have some cover for their heads, too. She also always brought along magazines that nobody ever seemed to get around to reading after all. Daddy used to say that getting Mother out on a picnic required as much gear as a trip to Europe.

Aunt Vivian had invited Audrey Dickenson and her mother to come along with us, and they appeared at the kitchen door just as I was helping Mrs. Lockley dry the last of the breakfast dishes. Blankets and magazines and even a few pillows that Mother had found and decided to take along were stacked on the little screened porch, ready to be carried out to the car, and Don and Ritchie were on their way outdoors with a bucket of ice.

"Hey, give us a hand, doll," Don said to Audrey,

and they both took her right on along out with them.

Mrs. Dickenson came into the kitchen to see if there were something she could do to help. (*Here, Mrs. Dickenson, I'll toss you my dish towel and you can dry the silverware while I run off and catch up with Ritchie Allen.*) But of course I only smiled politely when Aunt Vivian introduced me as her "darling niece, Louise," and said what an angel I was, always willing to help.

Mrs. Dickenson looked quite a lot like Audrey, very black-haired and tall. She had a supply of pillows and blankets under her arms, which I knew Mother would be delighted to see; and she was wearing a broad-brimmed straw hat, although it was still cloudy and showed little signs of turning into an overly sunny day. Aunt Vivian had told her not to bring a speck of food, but she had brought a big box of doughnuts that must have been fresh from the bakery because at once they could be smelled all over the kitchen. Everyone commented, "Oh, how good those smell!"

But then when we were finally all ready and the very last thing had been put into the cars, Mrs. Lockley began to look very much alone in the kitchen, empty now of every pickle and banana and boiled egg, every box and dish and carton that had been strewn everywhere such a little while before.

Except for Aunt Vivian, I was last to go out, carrying the chocolate cake with the utmost care, and I stopped and looked back as I heard Aunt Vivian ask

Mrs. Lockley if she wanted to go home. "I guess there isn't any reason you need to stay here all day," Aunt Vivian said. "We won't be back until evening. When you finish up in the kitchen, why don't you go home for the rest of the day."

Mrs. Lockley looked around a moment uncertainly. The ironing board had been set up the night before, and a wicker basket of clothes stood beside it.

"Oh, the ironing," Aunt Vivian remembered aloud. "Well, there's no reason why that can't be done tomorrow."

"All right," Mrs. Lockley said, folding her thin, wrinkled fingers in front of her flat stomach and long, serviceable apron. "Thank you, Mrs. Ellison, maybe I will go on home."

She looked around again, a little nervously, I thought—but with a certain relief that she did not have to spend all day alone in that house.

I couldn't help thinking about her as we drove along toward the river. I could see her in my mind's eye, spreading the dish towels to dry on the top of the stove, taking off her apron, putting it carefully on the ironing board or the back of a chair, neatly, so it wouldn't be wrinkled next time she put it on. I could almost see her going through the house to check that the front door was locked, and the terrace doors. Then back to the kitchen pantry, where she kept a flat little brown hat on a shelf—on with the hat, a sweater over her arm, stepping through the kitchen door to the screened porch, locking the door behind her. I could see her going across the porch and down the steps, walking along the side of the house— where the cars had all left the driveway now—to the front lawn and on out to the street. Drawing her breath with deep relief to find herself securely upon the public road and no longer alone (or worse, not alone) in that house.

At the river we did all the things we usually did on our picnic each summer: swam, ate on blankets spread on the grass, and walked through the woods, along the trail that never seemed to change from summer to summer, up to the highway and the little filling station and the grocery there to buy ice cream. We walked along strung out like Indians in file, Don and Audrey and Jessie and me and Marcella and Ritchie; and I thought how many years it was since we had first come along that trail to buy ice cream and how far the walk had seemed then to our little legs, and how dense and full of mystery the woods had seemed.

Off and on as the day passed, I thought about the house, empty, silent, locked up tight. I thought of tree branches touching windows, brushing and scraping and looking in with fluttering, whispering leaves; I thought of children riding by on bicycles, of a mailman, perhaps, coming up the walk and pushing mail through the slot so it would fall inside on the polished hall floor—observed only by the clock and the chandelier and the shining banister of the stairway. I thought of the worn old steps that led down into the cellar I had never seen; and I thought of the birdbath in the garden suddenly darkened by some strange reflection peering in—and bushes breaking as a black cat came through and sat upon the lawn.

When we came back to the house I looked for a change, a sign—and yet I did not know what change there could be or what sign I expected. The basket of ironing stood beside the board exactly as we had left it that morning; Mrs. Lockley's apron was folded neatly on a chair; the dish towels had dried on the stove top.

If I could have gone in alone and not broken the stillness and the half-light of early evening, I might have found a change, a sign, but at once the house was filled with the sound of all our voices and foot-steps; the noise of picnic baskets being set down; dishes clinking out onto the porcelain tabletop; the empty cake plate; the pickle jar; the saltshakers. Uncle Arthur switched on lights. Mrs Dickenson and Audrey hovered among us, and everyone was sud-denly thirsty and tired and dirty, leaving blankets and pillows, straw hats and magazines, empty ice bucket, empty lemonade bottles, and extra sweaters on the porch in a jumble.

More lights came on, as gradually we swarmed through the house, until even upstairs there were lights as Jessie ran up to bring Aunt Vivian a pair of slippers.

If there was some sign, I could not find it—nor did

I know exactly why I looked for one. It was only that the house had been alone all day and now we were all back. And the stone horses in the garden were silent and would not tell the secret.

In the morning Uncle Arthur announced that he had found a buyer for the house—or, more exactly, that someone who had called a week before and inquired about the house had definitely decided to buy it. Uncle Arthur made this announcement to everyone at the breakfast table, after receiving a telephone call which he took in the library. He came back into the dining room rubbing his hands together and looking jolly and satisfied. A pale sun sent first growing, then diminishing light through the windows, as the clouds refused to relinquish the sky completely; but it was a considerable improvement on the bleak grayness of the three days just past.

"Well, it's all settled," Uncle Arthur said to Aunt Vivian and gave a brisk nod.

"That was Mr. Trevor on the phone?" she asked eagerly. "Oh, it will be such a relief to sell the house before we go and not have that to worry about while we're trying to get settled in a new place. Oh, I *am* glad."

She looked around at us all and elaborated for our benefit. "There was a man quite interested last week. He came and looked around and said he'd let us know. But I didn't want to count on him—you know how it is."

"He's made up his mind for sure now," Uncle Arthur said. "We're supposed to meet him at Hansen's office at eleven."

"Ah!" Aunt Vivian let her breath out in a long, happy sigh.

"Mr. Trevor?" Jessie asked incredulously. "Mr. *Trevor*?"

"Yes. What *is* the matter, Jessie?" Aunt Vivian stared across the table at Jessie curiously.

"Where was *I* when he came and looked at the house?"

"Oh, out riding your bike, I think." Aunt Vivian gestured vaguely.

"Mother, don't you remember the legend—John Trevor was the man who jilted Catherine Isherwood. Don't you remember? They were engaged and all of a sudden he ran off and married someone else."

"It certainly can't be the same Mr. Trevor," Uncle Arthur answered calmly, if a little absently. "This man is only about forty years old."

"Mrs. Lockley said John Trevor is dead anyway," Jessie interrupted.

"Well that's something." Aunt Vivian gave a little sigh. "We won't have to worry anymore about *that* Mr. Trevor anyway—unless he comes back to haunt the place too, like what's her name."

"Like Catherine Isherwood," Jessie said.

"Never mind," Aunt Vivian said, less patiently. "That's enough talk like that."

"What is it?" Mother asked politely; it reminded

71

me of one of her club ladies saying sweetly, "How does the recipe go for these lovely cookies?"

"Oh, it's a long story, I'm afraid," Aunt Vivian answered. "But to be brief, some girl who once lived in this house was deserted by her fiancé. She is supposed to have died at sea and then come back to haunt this house."

"With her cat," Jessie put in persistently.

"With her cat," Aunt Vivian repeated eloquently, to show this proved her point and made the story even less believable.

"But Louise saw the cat in the garden," Jessie said.

And everybody looked at me.

"I did," I began timidly. All the grown-ups seemed so skeptical that I could even persuade myself that the shadow on the stairs had not been there after all. I felt that they were once again moving me into Jessie's age-group—and Marcella sat forward, hand cupping her chin, to see what I would say next.

"I saw a black cat around here, too," Ritchie said, and everybody looked at him and for the moment forgot me.

"You did?" Aunt Vivian paused and then shrugged. "I suppose there probably is some stray around here. Maybe Mrs. Lockley's been feeding it —or Mrs. Dickenson next door. You know, if you feed cats they never go away."

"Where did you see it?" Jessie asked.

"I saw it yesterday when we were putting things in

72

the car for the picnic," Ritchie said. He smiled at me. "It's the same one Louise saw, I guess—from the way she described it. It was very big, and all black. It was under the porch steps, but when it saw me it ran away."

"Under the porch steps?" Aunt Vivian sounded nervous to think the cat was so close and nobody was even sure that it existed. "What would it be doing under the steps?" she demanded of Uncle Arthur.

Uncle Arthur said, "I'm sure I don't know. Shall we tell Mr. Trevor that he's not only buying a house, but a legend and a ghost and a black cat?"

"I wonder if he likes cats," Mother said lightly.

But Aunt Vivian did not look amused. She studied Ritchie Allen gravely. It was one thing to chide Jessie for making up things and letting her imagination run away with her; it was one thing, even, to listen to what I said with reservations; but certainly nobody could doubt that Ritchie Allen had seen a cat if he said he had. He looked back at us all steadily from his dark eyes under the dark tumble of hair.

But then Jessie startled everybody by exclaiming loudly, "Mr. Trevor is probably John Trevor's son. Mrs. Lockley said John Trevor had a couple of children. Couldn't it be him—a son, I mean?" She turned to Uncle Arthur to see what he would say.

"Well, now, I don't know. Trevor isn't an unusual name," Uncle Arthur began hesitantly.

"Ask him, Daddy," Jessie begged. "Ask him when you see him this morning."

"Jessie, that's enough nonsense." Aunt Vivian pushed back her chair and stood up.

"But, Mother, if he is the son, something terrible will probably happen if you sell him this house."

Uncle Arthur threw back his head and laughed. Jessie's face flushed red with embarrassment and anger.

"It will *too*, Daddy," she said, and across the table our eyes met and held. *We knew*, we thought, Jessie and I—*we knew*; but it wasn't our fault that no one believed or cared or listened.

We went into the kitchen after breakfast and told Mrs. Lockley about the man who was going to buy the house. From the side window we could see Uncle Arthur and Aunt Vivian getting into the car in the driveway and starting off toward the real estate office to meet Mr. Trevor and sign the papers to sell the house.

Mrs. Lockley came and stood and watched out of the window too, arms crossed, her face gloomy in an inscrutable way.

"Something will happen, won't it, Mrs. Lockley?" Jessie asked.

Mrs. Lockley nodded. "I expect it will," she said.

CHAPTER SEVEN

ALL MORNING Jessie and I waited for Uncle Arthur and Aunt Vivian to come back and tell us whether the Mr. Trevor who was going to buy the house was the son of John Trevor, who had so long ago run off and married Ellen Alton.

We watched Ritchie and Don set off with Marcella and Audrey Dickenson to play tennis at the Westriver Park courts, without thinking to invite us or giving us a backward glance as they drove off in Daddy's car . . . I thought of Catherine Isherwood with her long, old-fashioned dress and a parasol, strolling along with John Trevor on a summer afternoon . . . and Catherine Isherwood gathering up her long, rustling skirts to run up the stairs, tears streaming down pale and beautiful cheeks—while in the hall below, looking upward after her, stood some neighbor or friend who had brought the news that John Trevor had married someone else.

I decided glumly that whatever else the house was it was unlucky for love affairs. It was a good thing my cousin Jessie was leaving before she got old enough to fall under that particular bad enchantment. I walked behind her through the hall to the library, studying her straight back and thin, sharp little shoulderblades that showed under the light cotton of her sundress, almost touched by the tips of straight, dark hair falling loosely about her shoulders.

It was past noon when Uncle Arthur and Aunt Vivian came back, and Mrs. Lockley was making sandwiches and iced tea for lunch. The day had grown hot and humid, despite the pale sunlight which struggled to shine through the light overcast.

Jessie and I were waiting in the front hall, and Aunt Vivian came in fanning herself with her handkerchief and looking warm. She could not help smiling a little to see us waiting there so eagerly.

"Yes, as a matter of fact, he *is* the son of John Trevor and Ellen Alton," she said. Her voice held a curious, speculative note, but she flourished her handkerchief again and dismissed her own words. "But that's beside the point; he's very happy about the house and we're very happy to have everything settled after all these weeks of uncertainty."

Uncle Arthur had come in behind Aunt Vivian and he nodded in agreement at what she said. He stood, hands in trouser pockets, looking over the house reflectively as though he were sorry to leave it but pleased that it was no longer a problem, that it had been sold.

"Mr. Trevor has been out of town for several years, and now he wants to return and settle down in the town where he was raised," Aunt Vivian explained. "His mother and father are dead, and his sister lives over in Garland. He says that he always liked this town and always wanted to buy a house here. Apparently he has done very well while he's been away. He's an architect. He'll appreciate all the good things about this house."

"Yes, he'll appreciate the house," Uncle Arthur said. He looked around again, nodding to himself so we could see he was glad that Mr. Trevor was a man likely to appreciate the house.

Jessie and I followed them out to the terrace, where Mrs. Lockley had brought sandwiches and cookies and iced tea. Mother and Daddy greeted us from behind newspapers and magazines, and Aunt Vivian and Uncle Arthur told them all about their morning's transactions. Before long, Don and Ritchie and Marcella and Audrey came back from the park, laughing, clumping their rackets along. Marcella, carrying a can of tennis balls, hardly looked ruffled; each hair was as perfectly in place as when she left, her lipstick as fresh, her tennis dress unwrinkled. Jessie, sitting on the arm of a lawn chair, twisted a long strand of hair and watched absently as they all trooped in and clustered around the umbrella table for sandwiches. Aunt Vivian took off her high heels and wandered around on the soft lawn inspecting the flowerbeds and sipping a glass of clear amber iced tea topped with a sprig of mint.

Don tossed me a tennis ball and we had a game of

catch until I missed the ball and it flew into the shrubbery that separated the lawn from the wall. I stood uncertainly beside the thick undergrowth of bushes and vines and tall grass, and then Ritchie came up beside me and said, "I'll get it for you," and pushed aside some of the low branches until we could see the ball by a twisted root of a thick bush. "Here it is," he said, crouching down and reaching for the ball.

A branch he had been holding out of the way snapped forward and scraped across his arm, leaving a long, deep scratch.

"Hey, these bushes fight back!" He laughed. "There."

He handed me the ball, and then rubbed at his arm until he caught me looking at him with concern and he said, "Hey, don't look like that. I think I'll live."

I lowered my eyes quickly and turned away—to show I didn't really care about his scratch. But by that time Don was talking with Audrey and Marcella, who were sitting on the iron bench on the terrace, and I put the ball into one of the cans by the terrace doors.

Ritchie stood a little apart from the rest, eating his sandwich and squinting into the hazy sun. I couldn't help watching him after all, and I thought about his rather lonely life, with his mother dead and his father traveling most of the time. I wondered if Ritchie minded being alone, and if he was happy

78

that my brother Don had brought him to our house at Christmastime and invited him to visit for the summer. I wondered if he was having a good time here with us now. Above his white cotton-knit shirt, his hair looked darker than ever; his eyes, with their long lashes, gazed with a faraway expression at thoughts I could only guess about—his father, perhaps; or his mother, whom he had never known. He had spent all his life at schools, and there did seem to be something almost wistful about him as he stood apart from us there in the garden. He seemed, just for a moment, a little like a stranger. But he wasn't a stranger—and never could be to me; I would always know his voice and I would always remember just how he looked, how he stood, how he walked—and how he smiled . . .

"Come and have something more to eat, sweetie," Aunt Vivian said, approaching with a tinkle of ice cubes in her empty tea glass. And she looked at me so kindly and wisely that I knew she had seen me staring at Ritchie Allen.

That afternoon Jessie and Marcella and I drove uptown with Mother and Aunt Vivian. Aunt Vivian had a few errands to do and Mother went with her. Jessie and Marcella and I browsed along Fullerton Street, looking in the store windows. It was still hot and sultry, but the sky had grown completely overcast again. The theater marquee flashed cheerfully and we strolled along slowly, deciding how we would spend the money that we had. Marcella had the most, and finally we went into *Ann's Dress Shoppe* with her and looked at dresses and lingerie. We all found something to buy, and when we met Mother and Aunt Vivian at the car we had to shift around to make room for ourselves and all the different packages there were with ours and Mother's and Aunt Vivian's all put together.

We were just managing to fit everybody and everything in, and Aunt Vivian was putting the key in the ignition, when she caught sight of a man passing by on the sidewalk.

"Hello there, Mr. Trevor," she called.

We all turned to look, and saw a nice-looking man with a small moustache and very gentle grayish-blue eyes. He was wearing a white suit and shoes and a straw hat. As he caught sight of Aunt Vivian he removed the hat to reveal a head that was almost bald except for a semicircle fringe of darkish hair that ran from ear to ear around the back of his head. He did not look in the least ominous or dangerous, and I nudged back as I felt Jessie poking her elbow into my side. He came a few steps nearer the car and said to Aunt Vivian, "I didn't think we would meet again so soon."

They both laughed, and Aunt Vivian said, "These are my guests—my sister, Mrs. Abbott, and my nieces, Louise and Marcella, and this is my daughter, Jessie."

To us she said, "This is Mr. Trevor, the gentleman who has bought the house."

"How do you do," Mr. Trevor said graciously and rather softly. He looked us over with a pleasant, quizzical expression, as though silently trying to figure out how we had all got in together with so many packages, and whether we would ever disentangle ourselves enough for all of us to get out again when we reached home.

We all murmured back politely to him, trying not to stare any more than we could help, and at last he backed away a step, nodding good-bye to us and saying, "It's been a pleasure to meet all of you."

But Aunt Vivian said, "We're having a buffet supper Saturday night. I wish you'd come, Mr. Trevor, and begin to get acquainted with your house."

"That would be very nice," Mr. Trevor said, "but I have a business engagement. I'm sorry."

"Oh, I am, too," Aunt Vivian said with disappointment. "Can't you change it?"

Mr. Trevor looked reluctant to refuse Aunt Vivian, but he shook his head helplessly. "I'm afraid not," he said. "I would love to come, I would indeed."

"We'd love to have you," Aunt Vivian said.

"I am sorry." Mr. Trevor looked sincerely regretful that he could not accept the invitation.

"Well, I can't say 'perhaps another time,' can I?" Aunt Vivian laughed. "This is our farewell party.

But you'll be having lots of company yourself when you live in the house, Mr. Trevor. It's a wonderful place for entertaining, you'll find."

"Oh, I'm sure it is," Mr. Trevor said. He remembered Jessie and Marcella and me in the backseat and included us in a gentle smile. "A nice place for parties for young people, too, I suppose."

Jessie stared back blankly, hypnotized by this contact with someone so close to the legend of Catherine Isherwood. But Marcella and I managed to keep up appearances by smiling and bobbing our heads.

"It's been a pleasure to meet you," Mr. Trevor said again, nodding his head and holding out his straw hat.

"I'm sorry you can't come Saturday," Aunt Vivian said. "Well, good-bye, Mr. Trevor." She put the key into the ignition and started the car.

"Good-bye," Mr. Trevor said, and he watched as we pulled away from the curb and drove off down the street. I looked back at him standing there, a dapper little man with his moustache trimmed just so, his round little bald head held in an elegant manner. It seemed strange to think that once, before he was born, his father had strolled up Plymouth Street—perhaps with a similar neat little moustache and elegant manner, but surely with more hair—to call upon Catherine Isherwood, who was so beautiful and rich and whose father was mayor of the town.

I had decided that I didn't like the John Trevor who had run off and married another girl; it seemed a mean and wicked thing to do, since he *was* engaged to Catherine Isherwood. But I found that I rather liked the bald-headed man with the straw hat in his hand who watched after us as we drove away down the street with our carful of parcels and Aunt Vivian's scarf billowing like a plume in the wind.

CHAPTER EIGHT

THE NEXT DAYS were full of preparations for the buffet supper on Saturday night. It was the grand finale, so to speak, of Uncle Arthur and Aunt Vivian's life in Westriver. Everything in the house was washed and polished, waxed and cleaned and arranged for the supper. Mrs. Lockley worked diligently along with Aunt Vivian and Mother, without actually permitting herself to feel festive about the affair; and often I would notice her pausing in her work to stare inscrutably into the garden.

The weather remained oppressively warm and humid. Occasionally a weary-looking sunlight would wash down on everything, bringing shadowy corners to light in the garden and making patches on the walk as it came through the tree branches.

On Thursday a gardener came. He was at work early in the morning when I looked out of the window in Jessie's bedroom, still yawning and blinking sleep out of my eyes. I watched him for a little while as he moved around, an old, bent little man with gnarled hands and a face burned dark by years of work outdoors.

"That's Mr. Benson," Jessie said, when she woke

and saw me watching him. "He comes every Thursday. He works next door at the Dickenson's on Fridays."

He worked in the garden until midafternoon, and when he had gone I asked Aunt Vivian why he didn't do anything to thin out the prickly bushes and stalks of plants that grew so thick along the wall.

"Oh, no, dear." Aunt Vivian looked shocked to think of such a thing. "That's supposed to be—well, rustic. That's part of the charm of the garden. Like a wildwood."

"Oh," I said.

When Mr. Benson had finished for the day, Aunt Vivian got Ritchie and Don busy stringing lights around the garden for the party.

But among the preparations for Saturday night there were a lot of ordinary, everyday things, too. Uncle Arthur and Daddy went off two days in a row to play golf. When Aunt Vivian and Mother were not doing something to get ready for Saturday night, they sat on the terrace or in the living room on the rose-colored sofas, talking and sipping iced tea or coffee. Audrey Dickenson seemed to come around a lot, tall and graceful, with her sleek almost-black hair circled with stretch bands of ribbon to match whatever outfit she was wearing.

Marcella and Ritchie Allen continued to find each other fascinating, and I watched them Friday afternoon walking in the garden when they thought no one was around. They were walking so close together

85

I couldn't have put a thin sheet of paper between them as they went along shoulder to shoulder.

Pointlessly, I tried to imagine what the week would have been like if only Aunt Vivian hadn't invited Marcella to come. I do not recall being bothered by guilty feelings at all as I calmly erased Marcella from the scene, in my mind's eye, turned her room back into a sewing room, and placed myself in the garden walking along with Ritchie Allen. Marcella, in my imagination, was safely at home in Albany, trotting out each day for her modeling lesson and bustling home with her model's box under her arm to help her mother in the hat shop. Or—in another, equally satisfying version—I imagined that Marcella had been invited to come for a visit, only after the first night in the spooky house, upon finding a book of ghost stories and a dead beetle for an omen of warning, she had quickly packed up her things and gone home again. *Good-bye, Marcella,* we all chorused as we saw her off on the Garland train.

Thus I sat, at Uncle Arthur's desk, the swivel chair turned to face the terrace doors and the strolling couple in the garden. Marcella was laughing up at Ritchie, and he was saying something to her. They made a perfect couple, Ritchie so dark and handsome, Marcella so blond and pretty and fashionable. I curled my legs under me in Uncle Arthur's big chair, swung it around away from the glass doors, and at last got up restlessly and went through the house looking for Jessie. She had dragged out her tile set again and was sitting in the kitchen with it, rather in the way, as Mrs. Lockley polished silver for the party Saturday night.

"Why don't we go swimming?" I asked, flopping down aimlessly beside Jessie at the kitchen table.

"It's going to rain," she answered, without even looking up from the tiles. Very steadily she held each one and daubed on the cement, then fastened it in its place on the tray. I watched her for a little while, and then Mother came looking for me to help in the dining room, where she and Aunt Vivian were unpacking extra dishes for the party. In one large box was a punch bowl and tray and eighteen cut-glass cups. I had the job of removing each from its wrapping of tissue paper.

"These have never been unpacked since we moved from the other house last fall," Aunt Vivian explained. "We thought we'd have so many years to entertain here, and now that we're leaving it seems we ought to use these things at least for the farewell party."

"They're all so lovely," Mother was exclaiming, as she unwrapped a silver tray and several silver candy dishes.

"Maybe it's silly," Aunt Vivian said. "They'll all have to be packed away again next week. Oh, I hate to think of all there will be to do."

"We'll stay and help," Mother offered impulsively. "Louise and I can stay. Charles has to go back Sunday, and he can take Don and Ritchie, and Louise and I will stay the extra week and help you. We can go home on the train."

"That would be wonderful—to have you both an extra week," Aunt Vivian said happily. "To say nothing of your help. If you're sure you can do it."

"Oh, I'm sure," Mother said. "Charles and the boys can easily manage without us for a week."

I didn't say anything, but I felt a little sad to think of Don and Ritchie going home with Daddy. When Mother and I did get home it would practically be time for Don and Ritchie to go back to school. I would hardly see Ritchie anymore at all. I carried the punch bowl and cups, in several trips, to the kitchen and helped Mrs. Lockley wash and dry them. Then we set them out on the dining-room sideboard, ready for Saturday.

It did begin to rain shortly, as Jessie had thought. And Ritchie and Marcella came in from the garden and got out the chess set in the library. Ritchie was going to teach Marcella to play, and after a reasonable time—so I would not look overanxious—I wandered into the library and sat down nearby to watch.

"It seems so complicated," Marcella said, rolling her eyes at Ritchie to show how smart she thought he was to understand chess. "I'm afraid I'll never learn."

"Sure you will," Ritchie said. After a moment he looked over at me and said, "Well, Little Miss Muffet, it's a good day for spiders."

"Are you trying to frighten me away?" I asked

88

icily. And he laughed as I got up and flounced over to the windows to watch the rain falling in thin streaks from the late-afternoon sky. In the garden the stone horses had dark spots made by the rain, and the iron bench had a wet shininess; the grass looked greener than ever and the flagstones darker, and all the flowers looked defenseless in the rain.

And then I saw the black cat sitting by the bird-bath, very straight and still, its tail curled around itself in a tight black circle.

Without saying anything to Ritchie and Marcella, who sat across the room behind me, a light turned on by their table, I opened the terrace doors and stepped out, as quietly and slowly and cautiously as I could. There was a chill in the air which had come with the rain, and I put my hands on my arms, hugging myself silently, and began to walk across the terrace toward the cat. Stealthily, taking a step and then a pause before the next step, I went across, heedless of the rain which fell on my hair and face and freshly ironed blouse. I was almost to the edge of the terrace, where the flagstones stopped and the lawn began, when the cat saw me. For a moment it seemed as though our eyes met and locked in some desperate, determined grip—like men with elbows braced on a table, struggling to see which can bend the other's arm down first to touch the table. And then the cat was gone—a streak of black across the grass and into the bushes—before I could draw a breath or make a move or utter a sound.

I stood rigid in my spot, unable to believe that the cat was gone so quickly, frightened to find myself suddenly out in the middle of the rainy garden, so far from the protection of the house, wet and bedraggled and as defenseless as the flowers. I whirled, feeling something pass close behind me—but there was nothing there, and then from the shelter of the library by the terrace doors I heard Marcella call, "Louise, what are you doing out there in the rain?"

I saw Ritchie beside her, starting out to meet me, and I ran back across the flagstones, hugging myself as though that would keep me warm or dry.

"Louise, look at you," cried Mother, who had chosen just that second to arrive in the library looking for a book. In the hall doorway behind her, Aunt Vivian appeared with a click of heels and a swish of skirts.

"Louise," she said, "you're all wet!"

It struck me so funny that I felt less cold and wet and frightened. They were all staring at me, and I said, "I thought I saw the black cat again. I just wanted to see how close I could get, to see if I could touch it, to see if it was real. But it ran away too fast."

"It's just some stray, not used to people," Aunt Vivian said, patting my damp shoulder. "Cats aren't as friendly as dogs, you know. They're very independent, I understand."

"Yes," Mother said. "Cats are very independent. You probably scared it, Louise."

90

"Yes," I said—wondering if any one of them heard the hint of irony in my voice. "I probably scared it."

As soon as I could slip away, I went to find Jessie and tell her I had seen the cat again. She gave me such unbroken, rapt attention and thought I was so brave to go out in the rainy garden alone to touch the cat, that I forgave her for being only twelve years old and obsessed with making a tray from colored tiles. She gave it up, anyway, for the rest of the afternoon, and hung around the windows looking into the garden to see if she could see the black cat herself. Or the ghost of Catherine Isherwood. Because I told her there was someone in the garden besides the black cat—someone or something that went by close to me, without touching me, but close enough so I knew someone was there. Except there had been nothing to see when I turned around.

On Saturday the sky cleared and Aunt Vivian flew about attending to all the last-minute details. Tables were set up on the terrace and folding chairs began to sprout up everywhere. The buffet was to be in the dining room and there were extra card tables to be set up in the living room and library in case of rain. Every room had vases of fresh flowers and dishes of candy and nuts.

Mr. Dickenson, whom I had not met before, came over with Audrey and Mrs. Dickenson, and they were the first to arrive. Aunt Vivian swished out to

91

meet them in a white lacy dress, and Jessie and I, coming downstairs, watched as she led them out to the terrace, where Mother and Daddy and Uncle Arthur had already gathered and fireflies were beginning to flicker in the dusky air. Marcella and Ritchie and Don and Audrey, paired off again so nicely, turned on the radio in the library and music floated out over the garden through the open terrace doors as they danced in the library. Jessie and I stood in the doorway watching them and the festive garden beyond, like two little children peeking at a forbidden Christmas tree on Christmas Eve.

Gradually the other guests arrived, perhaps twenty-five or thirty in all, and there were people everywhere through the house, from Mrs. Lockley's kitchen to the terrace, and all the rooms between. Another woman had come to help Mrs. Lockley, a stout, red-faced woman who worked very hard in the kitchen and seemed to be very happy about everything. Everyone ate and talked and wandered around, dancing in the library and on the terrace. Lamps glowed on the dark places of the lawn where I looked for shadows moving and saw nothing but deepening darkness as night came.

It was almost ten o'clock when Mr. Trevor came. Most of the food had been cleared away from the long dining-room buffet. Candles had been placed there, and the punch bowl and the cut-glass cups and two great high fancy cakes. Jessie and I had each fixed ourselves a second helping of cake (feeling it was only right to have one piece of each kind) and we were carrying our plates and punch cups through the hall to join the others dancing in the library, when the doorbell chime made a feeble sound, almost lost in the music and chatter of voices through the house. A group of grown-ups, who had taken over the rose-colored sofas in the living room to discuss the terrible state of the world, talked on undisturbed. I waited in the middle of the hall as Jessie answered the door. Holding her cake and punch cup precariously in one hand, she managed to get the front door open and stood squarely before it in consternation at the sight of Mr. Trevor standing there. At that moment a streak of lightning cut across the darkness, lighting up the sky behind him until he stood there silhouetted in the doorway. Following close upon the lightning was the sound of low, still-distant thunder. I stood there stupidly, holding my cake and punch cup and staring at Mr. Trevor as though he had three heads or six legs. He looked somewhat surprised himself, to see us there gaping so dumbly at him over our cake plates.

"I beg your pardon," he said graciously. "I have startled you. I'm sorry."

Jessie looked around at me over her shoulder, and I smiled back weakly.

Mr. Trevor said, "I hope I'm not too late to enjoy at least some of Mrs. Ellison's party. I found I was able to get away from my business appointment earlier than I expected."

He was wearing a dark suit and shoes—and looked, if possible, even more dapper and elegant than before. The gold bar of his tie clip sparkled as it caught the light.

"Come in," Jessie said, recovering her senses at last and stepping back out of the way.

Mr. Trevor sensed that we were ill at ease for some reason, and he looked genuinely concerned, almost as though with any slight encouragement from us he would have offered to help us with whatever it was that troubled us so.

"Umm. Mother and Daddy are out there." Jessie nodded toward the library and terrace beyond. Dancing couples moved by the doorway amid light and music, as yet unbothered by signs of an approaching storm. But Jessie and I noticed that a strong wind was now coming in through the door she had opened for Mr. Trevor—it ruffled the full skirts of our dresses and blew a paper napkin that someone had dropped back along the hallway toward the kitchen.

Jessie closed the door and, looking around at me for assistance, offered to show Mr. Trevor out to the terrace where Aunt Vivian and Uncle Arthur were. "Unless you'd like some cake and punch first," she said, recalling her duties as hostess.

"Thank you, no," Mr. Trevor said. "I'll just step out and see your mother and father. Don't trouble yourselves; I'm sure I can find them."

And with that he left us standing there and made

his way alone through the dancers in the library to the terrace doors, and we could no longer see him as he mingled with the people there. We followed into the library slowly, and another low rumble of thunder sounded, not quite so far off as the first. Flickers of lightning played across the sky, and now through the terrace doors there was a wind coming that even the dancers noticed, and they turned to look out toward the garden.

The storm seemed to break all around us with no warning more than the distant rumbles of thunder and the strong wind through the doors. Before anyone could act, paper plates and napkins blew from terrace tables, women's fluffy, bouffant party skirts billowed about their knees, and the terrace doors slammed shut from some force of vacuum created by the wind—but not before papers had blown off Uncle Arthur's desk, and a strong, dazzling flash of lightning lit up the whole night and the scurrying guests and windblown garden for a long moment that was full of an eerie unrealness, followed by darkness and the horrible deafening crash of thunder, close now, directly over our heads, hurling the rain in a sweeping torrent from the terrible sky above.

Everything seemed to bend and struggle and writhe under the force of the rain and the wind. Trees bent down low over roof and wall and garden, and in another minute there was nothing dry to be seen outside at all, so quickly was everything drenched and dripping with the rain. The stone horses sprang into view with another blaze of lightning that cut down from the darkness, and with wings raised they seemed about to fly off into the wild night. Somewhere something broke with a crash and tinkle of glass—an open upstairs window, or a dish knocked from a table to the terrace flagstones. And from some window or door still open came a draft of air that tortured the candles and kept at them until they sputtered out.

Jessie and I stood side by side, our cake plates forgotten in our hands.

It was the most terrible and the most sudden storm that I had ever seen; and I trembled with fear and cold at every sound of thunder or bolt of light in the sky. It seemed that it went on forever, and when it stopped at last, the garden lay in ruins in the darkness.

CHAPTER NINE

MOTHER AND I stayed on the next week to help Aunt Vivian in her preparations to move.

The ravages of the garden were only partially guessed at during the night of the storm, but they sprang fully and hideously into view on the following morning. It was Sunday, and church bells chimed over Plymouth Street and over the town. A haze in the air melted away under a fairly warm sun.

There lay the garden, with every flower beaten down flat to the ground, petals pounded into the muddy earth, torn from the heads of the flowers. Ivy had been caught by the wind and ripped from the wall in patches that dangled limply to the ground. Bushes and small trees were flattened, and leaves lay everywhere, stripped from every tree and plant by the wind and rain. At one side of the garden a tree had been split evenly down the middle by lightning and stood opened like some blooming monstrosity with giant petals made of the sides of the tree.

Everywhere was the debris of the party—plates and glasses, napkins, food, a handkerchief and a pair of white gloves lost by guests in their hurry to get indoors when the storm broke.

We all stood shocked and awed by the sight, and not one of us could dream that it was only a small part of what was eventually to come. Aunt Vivian was the first to retreat, shaking her head hopelessly as she went back into the house. "What an end to our lovely party," she said. "What an end to our lovely party."

"It certainly was a lovely party," Mother said, following Aunt Vivian and trying to sound cheerful. "I know everyone had a wonderful time."

"I never saw any storm come on so fast," Uncle Arthur said to Daddy.

"No," Daddy agreed, "neither have I."

Ritchie and Don went out on the squishy wet grass and explored around the broken bushes and destroyed flowerbeds. Then Don got a wastebasket from the kitchen and they began picking up plates and napkins and things. Jessie and Marcella and I helped, and we all worked away on that peaceful, sun-fresh Sunday morning, while the Sunday bells chimed over the town. We worked in a quiet, subdued way, until we had everything picked up and all the extra chairs folded and stacked by the side of the house. The umbrella had come loose from its fastening over the metal table, and although Don and Ritchie worked at it awhile they could not get it back securely again, and it hung at a lopsided angle and flopped threateningly if anyone jarred the table.

The garden looked frightening, I thought—battered and desolate, as though it was somehow dying on that bright day while the bells were ringing.

When we went back into the house at last, Mrs. Lockley had breakfast on the table and we sat down, but no one felt much like eating.

Daddy and Don and Ritchie were packed and ready to leave for home, and they were on their way soon after breakfast. Daddy had to be in his office Monday morning. We waved as they pulled out of the driveway, and I wondered if Audrey Dickenson in her house next door minded that Don was going home and she would never see him again. No, I thought, looking across the drive and up to windows of the Dickenson house that I could see over the tips of trees, Audrey was probably in her room with her back to us, laying out her beautiful new clothes and thinking about college. I thought that because she was eighteen and grown-up and going away to college she could never miss a boy, like I would miss Ritchie.

I wasn't the only one who missed Ritchie. I noticed a certain amount of interest in visiting Aunt Vivian and Uncle Arthur fell away from Marcella after Ritchie left. She couldn't seem to find anything she really wanted to do, and two days later she went home herself. Jessie and I drove over to the Garland station with Uncle Arthur to put her on the train. "Good-bye, Marcella," we all called, like I had imagined we called in my daydream; but now it was too late. Ritchie Allen, with his beautiful dark eyes and tumbling dark hair, had gone first, so it didn't matter anymore.

As the week passed, Jessie finished her tile tray, and Mother and Aunt Vivian packed books and dishes and clothes. One afternoon a Mrs. Henderson came around to visit Aunt Vivian and she claimed the pair of gloves we had found in the garden the morning after the storm. She was a plump, pink woman with tiny feet and fat little fingers, and she examined the handkerchief we had found on the lawn, but said it wasn't hers.

"Someone will remember it and be around for it," she assured us.

But no one ever did claim it, although everyone who had been at the party either called on the telephone during the week, or stopped in at the house to say one last good-bye to Aunt Vivian and Uncle Arthur.

"It seems fragile, as though it was old," Mother said, examining the delicate, deep edging of lace—and that was what started Jessie and me being so interested in it. We always remembered to ask Aunt Vivian's visitors if they had lost a handkerchief the night of the party, and we sometimes brought it from the hall table for their inspection if they looked uncertain.

But when they saw it, they always said it wasn't theirs. And we would take it back and put it on the hall table, exchanging looks just between ourselves to show that we were not really surprised that it hadn't been claimed.

We thought it belonged to the ghost of Catherine Isherwood, and we asked Mother if it could be fifty years old.

"I suppose it *could* be," Mother said. "Some things last quite well. But it would probably have a yellowish cast if it were *that* old."

"I remember that Arthur's mother's wedding dress fell to shreds when we lifted it out of the box in the attic when we moved from the other house," Aunt Vivian said. "It was about fifty years old. But his father's wedding coat was in good enough condition to be worn by someone, if it hadn't been so out of style."

Mrs. Lockley didn't like the handkerchief—nor the ravaged garden. She moved more silently than ever about the house and in the kitchen, starting nervously at sudden sounds and occasionally dropping a spoon or a pot holder as she went about her work.

"What will you do when we go, Mrs. Lockley?" Jessie asked her one afternoon.

"I'll probably take another housekeeping job," she answered, with a barely perceptible pause.

"Maybe you could just stay on here," Jessie said. "Maybe Mr. Trevor will need a housekeeper. He's not married, you know. In fact, he's sure to need one. This is such a big house, he'll need somebody."

But Mrs. Lockley shook her head. "I'll finish out

the week here, and that's all," she said flatly. "I'd go now, but your mother needs me."

"Why would you go now?" I asked apprehensively, pushing back bangs from my warm forehead and studying her intently.

"Never mind," she said. "I'll stay until the week's out, until my time's up with Mrs. Ellison. I wouldn't leave her now, with all the packing and things she has to do."

But Mrs. Lockley was anxious to get away. She seemed to leave earlier in the evenings and to hurry through her work to be sure it was all done in shorter time. She made it very clear to us that she did not want anything more to do with the house—especially with Mr. Trevor coming.

Mr. Trevor telephoned the morning after the storm to ask how everything was, and Uncle Arthur reported the damage in the garden and the tree that had been struck by lightning. Mr. Trevor said he would be around for a look during the week if he could, but he had a very pressing week before him, and as it turned out he didn't come again while we were there.

It was warm that week, and Jessie and I went swimming twice in the park pool; and I thought about it being the last time we would ever visit Uncle Arthur and Aunt Vivian in this particular town, the last summer I would ever come to the West-river Park pool. The cement steps coming up from the shower rooms to the pool deck were cool and rough, and sunlight broke above us. Below was the steamy, chlorinish smell of the dressing rooms and showers, the sound of little children laughing and the jangle of the matron's keys, evoking memories of myself the first time I had come there, aged nine or ten, pattering along across the wet shower-room floor, holding little Jessie by the hand and looking around when we came upstairs to find Don, who was big enough to take care of us both.

Now as we came up the stairs at the deep end of the pool, college boys practiced dives from the high board and Jessie and I were old enough to dive in from the side and race across the width of the pool and back again, while little children splashed on the other side of the middle rope, and sleepy sunbathers lay along the sidelines. But it would have been so much more fun with Don and Ritchie . . . Jessie and I walked home through the park and along quiet, shady streets, carrying our towels and suits in beach bags and feeling our hair to see if it was getting dry.

Gradually that week the house took on an empty look, with books and bric-a-brac packed away, and curtains down in most of the rooms. However, there were certain furnishings that Aunt Vivian and Uncle Arthur had sold to Mr. Trevor along with the house. In the living room, a specially made draw drapery that closed across the entire length of the front windows was to be left, as well as draperies in the library and master bedroom upstairs. Carpeting in the living room, dining room, and bedrooms was to be left; and so even on the very last day, when the movers came for the furniture and barrels of dishes and boxes of books and clothes, the house was not entirely bare.

That last night I looked out from the window in Jessie's room, down upon the walled garden lighted by a moon, and it was almost beautiful again with the soft light over everything and only the sound of leaves stirring in a night wind that was high up in the branches.

But in the morning the wind was gone. There was an absolute dead calm, and a silence in the air I had never been aware of before. It was a hush like a warning, a hush that made you strain to hear something that was only more silence, stretching out into infinity around you.

We had a rather odds-and-ends breakfast at the kitchen table, which Aunt Vivian had decided to leave for Mr. Trevor (having her heart set on a modern new kitchen in California), and after we had eaten, Aunt Vivian told Mrs. Lockley to take home anything that was left over that she wanted.

"There are some eggs and a pound of butter in the refrigerator," Aunt Vivian said. "And there's almost a whole loaf of bread here in this cupboard." She looked sleepy and pale and jittery, and she had on a gray sweater that she kept pulling closer around her as if she were cold.

Uncle Arthur had eaten earlier, and he was putting suitcases and bags in the car, and while we were still eating, the movers were going up and down the stairs taking out furniture. Jessie and I hurried through breakfast so we could go and watch. I suppose we were in the way, but the movers were good-natured and they acted like they enjoyed having an audience. They kept mopping their faces with big square handkerchiefs and carrying out tables and chairs and boxes. At last there was no place to sit but on the stairway or the iron bench in the garden.

And the calm persisted; not one leaf moved on any tree, not one breath of air stirred, not one sound came to us from the world on the other side of the wall.

In the library the men carried out Uncle Arthur's desk with the drawers tied shut; and the globe; and the leather chairs. Then Aunt Vivian came to find Jessie and me, sitting on the iron bench.

"We can go now, girls," she said, and for the last time the three of us stood on the terrace looking around at the strange, still garden where sky reflected in the birdbath but there were no birds.

One of the moving men came to the terrace doors to ask Aunt Vivian about something, and Jessie and I went back to the kitchen to say good-bye to Mrs. Lockley. But Mrs. Lockley had gone. The kitchen was empty and her hat was gone from the shelf. Cupboard doors hung open to reveal bare shelves. The door to the cellar was open and I could see down the worn old steps into a shadowy dark depth that I had never explored.

"Come on, Louise." Jessie tugged at my arm, and

we hurried back to the front of the house, our footsteps echoing loudly in the empty house on the bare polished hall floor. The movers were taking out the last few things under Aunt Vivian's final directions. Uncle Arthur's car stood in front of the house, and Mother and Uncle Arthur were already outside waiting for us.

Uncle Arthur and Aunt Vivian and Jessie were going to drive Mother and me to the train station in Garland, where we would get a train for home, and Daddy would meet us at the other end. Then they were going to begin the drive to California, to their new house.

Uncle Arthur drove slowly along the familiar streets of Westriver, and we were all quiet, looking through the car windows as well-loved places slipped past, never to be seen again. Moving was the oddest-feeling thing in the world, I thought; I was glad it wasn't our family that was moving, leaving behind a town we had lived in as long as I could remember. Jessie sat hunched toward the window, head forward, to be sure that she did not miss the last glimpse of anything. Slowly we wound through the streets and out to the highway that ran to Garland. Uncle Arthur had put the convertible top up, so it would not be too windy for Mother, who was riding with Jessie and me in the backseat, and we sped along in the still morning over a deserted road, passing only a few horses grazing in a pasture and farmhouses looking aloof behind their fences and fields.

106

In the Garland depot we all got out of the car and bought root beer from an automatic dispenser inside the station. The stationmaster was eating his lunch behind his window grating, a sandwich in wax paper and a thermos of coffee. We went outside and strolled up and down the brick station yard, squinting down the track to see the train, and in the station house the phone rang four or five times before the stationmaster reluctantly set aside his sandwich and shuffled to answer it.

He came to the doorway and called over to Uncle Arthur, "You Mr. Ellison?"

"Why, yes." Uncle Arthur looked surprised.

"It's for you then," the stationmaster said. We all went inside, and he handed the phone to Uncle Arthur, withdrawing to watch curiously, as I suppose some note of urgency had been conveyed to him in the caller's voice.

It was Mrs. Lockley—calling to tell us that the house in Westriver was burning down. I remember, in that instant before we all ran to get into the car again, how we exchanged speechless, open-mouthed looks, and how the stationmaster peered out at us through his window, munching his sandwich and watching as we drove away again without waiting for our train.

"Burning!" Aunt Vivian came to life first as the car pulled out of the station with a screech of tires that would have thrilled my brother Don and Ritchie Allen. "How can it be burning?"

Uncle Arthur had not revived yet, and he only shook his head in confusion and gunned the car off along the highway at a furious speed.

"Burning!" Mother echoed Aunt Vivian. "How can it be burning?"

"Arthur, what else did Mrs. Lockley say?" Aunt Vivian gasped, as the farms sped away behind us and the horses grazing in their pasture hardly had time to look up before we were already by them and out of sight.

"She said Audrey Dickenson telephoned her as soon as the blaze was discovered. Mrs. Lockley said it was burning, everywhere, in every room. The fire engines are there, all of them I guess—and I suppose everybody in town, too."

He was right. What a sight greeted us as we came down Plymouth Street! We could not get within two blocks of Uncle Arthur's house—though it was not his house anymore; it was Mr. Trevor's house now.

It looked like everyone in town had come to see the fire. Fire equipment and cars lined several blocks on both sides of the house, and we were forced to leave Uncle Arthur's car at last and go on foot, pushing our way through the crowds. Hoses were stretched across the street, and firemen swarmed over the drive and garden. Flames burned in every room, burst from every window; and at the back of the house, over the kitchen and screened porch, part of the roof fell in and a plume of smoke and flame rose up as the roof went in with a horrible sucking,

108

crushing sound. Black debris showered out and several onlookers stifled screams. Women clutched their children closer, and the men talked to each other without taking their eyes from the house.

But there was nothing the firemen could do. The fire had started (although everyone said that was impossible) in every room at once. Draperies at living-room and upstairs windows were seen flaming by someone passing in the street. By then the movers were gone, and the house was entirely empty. But before the alarm was turned in and the fire trucks could come, the fire was already so far advanced that the firemen could not go in at all, and they helplessly sprayed water from outside to keep the fire from spreading, while inside everything burned black and crisp, stairways crumbled, and the upstairs floor fell in on the rooms below.

It burned until the stone fireplace and chimney stood scarred black in the smoking ruins of the once-fine house, and in the garden two stone horses with wings, an iron bench, and a birdbath stood on a trampled, torn-up lawn and terrace strewn with charred wood and broken glass and the black ashes of the fire.

As I watched, I saw the days of my visit unfolding before me like pages of a book ruffling backward— the movers carrying out the furniture; Mr. Trevor standing in the doorway with the lightning shooting through the sky behind him; the beetle lying on the cover of *Ghost Tales*; the rain falling against the terrace doors; Jessie licking pink icing from her fingers and saying, "Mrs. Lockley, tell Louise about the ghost"; and Aunt Vivian coming to greet us with arms outstretched and high heels clicking on the polished floor.

CHAPTER TEN

IT HAS BEEN five years since that summer, five years since Uncle Arthur and Aunt Vivian and Cousin Jessie left Westriver, New York, and moved to California to live.

We don't go to see them every summer, as we did when we were children; as the years pass, everyone seems to get busier and scattered around in different places (I went to two summer sessions at college, and Don accepted a job with Ritchie Allen's father and travels most of the time nowadays, which gives him a nice wide range for his favorite activity— breaking girls' hearts); and California is so much farther to travel to, of course.

But we did go once, about two years after they moved, and we admired their new house and all the wonders of California. Jessie was fourteen then, and had a boyfriend who hung around the house saying silly things to her and lapsing into a tongue-tied silence whenever anyone said anything to him.

Jessie is seventeen now, and from the last picture Aunt Vivian sent us I see that Jessie has her hair in a very short, stylish cut, high on top and tucked behind the ears. She has graduated from high school and is busy getting ready for college now, and she doesn't like to be called Jessie anymore, but Jessica—which she feels is more appropriate for being seventeen and going away to college.

She writes me sometimes, and her most recent letter came a few days ago, on a hot August morning, and was put with the rest of the mail on the hall table.

My summer job consists of doing some typing for Daddy at his office. But on the day Jessie's letter arrived I had slept late because it was my day off; when I finally came downstairs Daddy was gone and Mother had left me a note saying that she was having her hair set at the beauty parlor and would be back by lunchtime.

I made myself some fresh coffee and a piece of toast, and sat on the porch and opened the letter from "Jessica." Out from the folded pages of my cousin's precise, clear writing came a page of paper yellowed by years, very fragile looking but in legible condition. I set it aside curiously, to read first what Jessie had written to me:

Dear Louise,

The other day I found this letter in a book we brought from the house in Westriver. It wasn't one of our books, but got packed by mistake with some really ancient things that were in the cellar and had been left there by people who had lived in the house before us.

112

The letter is from Catherine Isherwood to her fa-
ther, while she was on her trip to Europe, and she
sounds pretty happy to me. I mean, not exactly as
though she were pining away too much for her lost
love or plotting anything horrible to do for revenge.
Read it and see what you think.

I guess I'll never forget that strange summer and
that awful fire—even though just about everything
that happened could be explained coolly and logi-
cally, as Mother is FOREVER reminding me!

(I could hear Aunt Vivian: *Now, Jessie, that cat*
was just a stray, and the storm the night Mr. Trevor
came was just a coincidence, and the fire was an acci-
dent—remember, the firemen said faulty wiring
could have been the cause in a house as old as that
one was, or one of the moving men might have left a
cigarette that wasn't put out, or a firebug might have
been watching the house, knowing we were all leav-
ing, and sneaked in when the movers left. And there
is probably some perfectly ordinary nice lady in
Westriver who just forgot that she left her best hand-
kerchief behind at our party. Mrs. Lockley was a
wonderful housekeeper, but she was inclined to be
superstitious about things. Everything can be ex-
plained simply and logically. And there are no such
things as ghosts!)

Aunt Vivian had said all those things the summer
that we visited her in California. And Mother and
Daddy and Uncle Arthur all agreed and nodded to

punctuate every sentence as Aunt Vivian went along.

But Jessie and I had never been fully persuaded, and at last we played our trump card, so to speak, by telling them about the shadow I had seen on the stairs. We hesitated to tell them even then, partly because we thought they might laugh at us and partly because we connected it with scaring Marcella, which we shouldn't have been doing in the first place. We didn't mention Marcella, and they didn't think to ask us what we were doing on the backstairs at one o'clock in the morning.

But even after we told them, it didn't change anything.

"It was just your imagination running away with you, Louise," Mother said. "Anybody can see strange shadows when they are in a strange house in the dark."

Perhaps they can—and perhaps that's all it was. But I can still feel the prickles of fear that ran up my arms when I heard that soft noise behind me. I can still remember pressing back against the wall and staring down at the dark shadow below me on the stairs.

As for scaring Marcella, I recall that with embarrassment, to think I had ever been so silly. And I like Marcella very much now. She comes with her mother to see us once or twice a year, and I don't feel jealous anymore because she is engaged to a nice boy who lives in Albany and I am engaged to Ritchie Allen with his long lashes and dark eyes and tumbling dark hair.

Ritchie is going to be a history professor and we will probably live near some small, peaceful college campus and go to faculty teas on Sunday afternoons.

He still calls me Little Miss Muffet and still tweaks my nose sometimes, but I don't mind that now. He says he can't exactly remember when he first stopped thinking of me as Don's little sister and began to fall in love with me, but he thinks it was that summer he went with us to visit Uncle Arthur and Aunt Vivian in Westriver. I think he is really wrong about that, for I surely do quite clearly remember how he spent most of his time looking dreamily at my cousin Marcella. But as long as he finally did stop thinking of me as Don's little sister, I guess it doesn't matter so much exactly when it was.

But I do remember the Christmas after that summer, when I had just turned sixteen. Ritchie came home with Don from school, and one night when we were helping Mother and Daddy trim the tree Ritchie kissed me in the hallway and said, "I don't think I need any mistletoe this time, do I?"

That whole Christmas holiday is one happy blur to me after that, and I really did get up the next morning and find that I had brushed my teeth and thrown my toothbrush into the wastebasket afterward, while I was under the enchantment of that kiss.

Carefully I unfolded the yellowing, aged letter,

which had been preserved between the pages of the book. It seemed unfair and prying to read it, a letter written so many years ago, exchanged between two people I had never known.

Dear Papa, it began. *We are having a wonderful time. Everything is so exciting and everyone is so nice to us. Mama says they love having American tourists here. We would hate to come home, except we miss you. I have bought some beautiful new dresses and Mama says we will have a big party as soon as we are home. We went to a lovely affair last night, and there were so many nice young men I hardly had a chance to catch my breath between dances.*

But we do miss you—Mama says to send you a kiss from her. We are sailing next week on Tuesday. Love, Catherine.

I read the letter over several times. Sunlight made a dappled pattern across the porch and on the table and on my hand holding the fragile, faded letter. I could hear birds calling in the trees around the house, and I could hear children shouting down the street somewhere. I felt in that moment connected with two worlds—my own world of that sunny summer street with birds chirping and children's voices in the distance; and that other world of so many years ago, the world in which Catherine Isherwood had lived . . . We are sailing next week on Tuesday, she had written, next week on Tuesday, next week on Tuesday, next week on Tuesday, to die in the cold, black ocean.

Jessie said the letter sounded happy. It did, I admitted to myself. Unless it was only bravado, Catherine Isherwood did not sound as if she were suffering from an irreparable broken heart or a thirst for revenge that would persist after her death and haunt the next fifty years of time. And if she really loved John Trevor, how could she have wanted to harm him, or any of his family, no matter how much he had hurt her . . . But the house *was* gone. Had Catherine Isherwood taken her revenge?—and in doing so destroyed the house she had loved and the only place she had to go . . .

I turned my attention back to finishing Jessie's letter, which concluded with a sketchy little drawing. I stared at it curiously for a minute before I realized what it was: she had drawn herself coming along the upstairs hall toward Marcella's room, wearing the bedsheet over her head; in an open doorway Marcella stood with arms upraised, eyes round as saucers, and mouth open wide for a scream —which was probably not so much the way she had looked but more the way Jessie had hoped she would look when she saw a specter advancing down the hall toward her; there was a picture of me, in my pajamas, crouching to hide across the hall and around the corner from Marcella's room, and behind me was an attempt to draw a stairway and

117

upon the stairway, a vague, dark shape in the shadows.

Under the picture Jessie had written, *If you remember this, I know you remember everything else as clearly as I still do.*

And she had signed the letter, *With Love, Jessica.*

I laid the two letters side by side on the table, and although sunlight moved upon them with a bright assurance that all was well, I felt once again the chill of fright that had filled me the night I saw the shadow on the stairs and all the times I had felt someone, something, watching me in empty rooms. I remembered the feeling of someone passing close to me on the rainy lawn—and the look of the black cat when our eyes met in a long, awful stare at one another.

I was not sure which was strongest, the reassurance of the sunny morning or the remembrance of a garden where there were no birds; and I sat on the porch looking off down the street to things that happened long ago. Everything Aunt Vivian said is so clearly logical; everything can be explained. But I know that black cats always startle me now, and I find myself wondering if they will vanish when I reach out to pet them . . . or if I will ever again see one sitting motionless in some unexpected place, watching me out of yellow eyes I have seen before.

118